Freddie reached too far for a peach and down came
little boy and all.

The Bobbsey Twins at Cloverbank

BY

LAURA LEE HOPE

AUTHOR OF "THE BOBBSEY TWINS SERIES,"

NEW YORK
GROSSET & DUNLAP
PUBLISHERS

Made in the United States of America

CONTENTS

THE BOBBSEY TWINS AT CLOVERBANK

CHAPTER I

THE MYSTERIOUS BOX

TAP! Tap! Tap!

Some one was knocking on the door of the kitchen where Dinah Johnson, the fat, jolly, colored cook of the Bobbsey family was just taking a pie from the oven. Holding the pie carefully, Dinah turned her head toward the door.

Tap! Tap! Tap! sounded again.

"Good lan' ob massy! Wonder who dat am?" murmured Dinah. "Maybe it am one ob dem woodpecker birds whut fly 'round de garden lookin' fo' bugs in de trees. But if Mistah Woodpecker t'inks he's gwine t' look at dis pie, he's mighty much mistook—dat's all I got to say!"

1

Dinah waddled over to the table, carrying the pie carefully, and then, as the knocking again sounded on the kitchen door, she walked toward it and opened it.

"Git away from heah, Mistah Woodpecker!" she exclaimed, before she really saw who it was. Then she started back in surprise, for Bert Bobbsey, carrying in his hands something wrapped in paper, slid quickly through the half-opened door and exclaimed:

"Don't tell Nan or Flossie or Freddie that I came in this way, Dinah! I want to get upstairs—quick!"

"Mah goodness! Bress yo' heart, honey! Has anyt'ing done happened dat yo' got to slip in in dis mysteriousness way an' hide upstairs? Whut's de mattah?" demanded the colored cook.

"Hush, please, Dinah! It's all right. I just don't want any of the others to know I came in this way!" explained Bert, with a smile, which told the cook that there was nothing very much wrong. "I'm going upstairs to hide this," Bert went on. "If Flossie comes in don't tell her you saw me."

"Oh—all right," remarked Dinah, with a chuckle. "Ah done guess it's some game dem Bobbsey twins is playin'," she went on to herself. "Bress der hearts! Nices' chilluns dat eber was! Dat's it! Some game Bert is playin' like hide de organ or find de auttymobile, Ah reckon! Ho! Ho!"

She laughed softly to herself as she waddled back to the oven to take out another pie, while Bert crept up the back stairs on tiptoe, still carrying the paper package of which he took great care.

"Dat's what it must be—some game!" murmured Dinah, and then, as she set the second pie on the table, again came the sound of knocking at the door.

"Go on away, Freddie!" went on Dinah. "Ah can't bodder wif yo' any more. Once is enough to come in mah kitchen when Ah's busy wif pies! Run along, Freddie!"

"Hush, Dinah, please!" came a voice from the outer side of the door. "This isn't Freddie. I'm Nan! Please open the door and let me in. I can't turn the knob—my hands are full!"

"Well, mah good lan' ob massy!" exclaimed the colored cook, as she gave a hasty look at the oven to make sure the third pie, still in the stove, would not burn. "Fust comes Bert, an' his hands is full; den comes Nan, an' her hands is full. Whut's gwine on in dish yeah house to-day Ah wonders?''

But remembering that Bert had begged her not to mention how he had entered, Dinah said nothing to Nan of this when she opened the door and saw Bert's twin sister standing there, holding in her arms a brown paper parcel, larger than the one Bert had carried up the back stairs.

"Thank you, Dinah, for letting me in," whispered Nan, with a smile. "This bundle is so big I couldn't reach the knob. Please don't tell Flossie or Freddie or Bert that I came in this way, will you?"

"No'm—Ah won't say one word!" promised Dinah, as she watched Nan tiptoe quietly up the back stairs.

Chuckling to herself, Dinah went back to the oven to get out the third pie, meanwhile having shut the outer kitchen door, for she did not want any draft of air blowing on her fresh pastry.

So she had closed the door and had set the third pie on the table when she was so startled that she gave a jump for, looking at one of the kitchen windows, she saw Freddie Bobbsey trying in vain to raise it. The window was partly open, but not wide enough for the little fellow to slip in.

"Dinah! Dinah! Open the window and let me in!" he begged. "And please hurry! It's very 'portant!"

"Um! It important, am it?" asked Dinah. "Den why doesn't yo' come in de do' laik de others done?" She meant Bert and Nan, but no sooner had she spoken than she remembered that the two older Bobbsey twins had each begged her to keep quiet about them. Luckily, however, Freddie did not pay much attention to the last part of Dinah's remarks.

"I don't want to come in the door 'cause Flossie will see me!" he explained, trying to wiggle under the partly raised sash. "She's out in the yard, watching, and I don't want her to see me. So open the window and let me in, please, Dinah!"

"Aw right, honey lamb, I will," promised the cook. "Dis suah mus' be some funny game de Bobbsey twins am playin'," she thought to herself. "An' Freddie's got a bundle, too! Dish suah am queer!"

Indeed, Freddie had a bundle. It was wrapped in a white cloth and was almost as large as himself, though it was not very heavy, for he lifted it easily into the window ahead of him, when Dinah had raised the sash higher.

"There! I guess Flossie didn't see me," murmured the little boy.

Instead of going up the back stairs as his older brother and sister had done, Freddie made for the cellarway which opened out of the kitchen.

"Where you going?" demanded Dinah, as she saw what the small lad was about to do.

"Hush!" he begged, holding a finger over his lips. "This is a secret! I want to hide it down the cellar. He'll never think of looking for it down there!"

"What is it?" asked the colored woman. "Who won't look down there for it? What is it, Freddie?"

But Freddie did not answer. He was going softly down the cellar stairs, carrying the package in cloth, almost as big as himself.

"If dis wasn't summer Ah suah would t'ink it was Christmus, wif everybody hidin' presents," Dinah murmured. "But Christmus don't come in June! It mus' be some game!"

She was just reaching for the tin can of powdered sugar which she intended sprinkling on the pies when a noise behind her caused her to turn quickly. She saw, tiptoeing out of the pantry, Flossie Bobbsey, Freddie's blue-eyed twin sister. Flossie, also, carried a good-sized package.

"Hello, Dinah!" murmured Flossie. "Those pies smell good!" and she hungrily sniffed the air. "But don't tell anybody you saw me!" she went on, with a smile, and she crossed the kitchen in the direction of a door that led to the back hall.

"Where'd you come from?" demanded Dinah. "I was in dat pantry a little bit ago an' you wasn't in it, Flossie!"

"I know!" giggled the little girl. "I got up on a box and crawled in the window. It was open. I didn't want Freddie to see me. He was out in the yard and I slipped away from him. I'm going to hide this in the little closet under the stairs," she went on, holding up the box she carried.

"What is it?" asked Dinah.

"It's a secret!" answered Flossie, with a smile. "Bert and Nan aren't around, are they?"

"No, they aren't 'round now," replied the cook.

"I'm glad of that," said Flossie, with a sigh of relief as she tossed her tangle of golden curls back out of her eyes. "I don't want any of them to know until we are at the table this evening."

"What's it all about?" asked Dinah, more from habit by this time than because she expected to be told. "Is it a game, honey lamb?"

"Sort of!" laughed Flossie. "But it's more of a secret!"

"Um! Yeah! I could guess dat part ob it!" chuckled Dinah. "It suah am a secret!"

She watched Flossie slip quietly out into the back hall and heard the little girl opening the small closet under the stairs, where all sorts of odds and ends were kept.

With a silent laugh, which shook her big, fat body as a bowl of jelly is shaken when it is placed on the table, the colored cook went on with her kitchen work. Soon she heard the voice of Bert as he went down the front stairs and out of the front door.

"Ah guess Nan didn't ketch him," murmured Dinah.

A little later, down the back stairway, floated the voice of Nan, speaking to her mother in the latter's room.

"An' Ah reckon Bert didn't see Nan," went on Dinah. "So far it's all right. Dat is ef dey don't ketch Flossie in de back hall."

But this did not happen, because Flossie remained in the little closet under the stairs for some time. She appeared to be taking great pains to hide the box she was carrying.

However, a little later Flossie came softly back into the kitchen through the door leading to the back hall.

"There! Nobody knows where it is but me!" she declared.

"Dat's good," murmured Dinah.

"And maybe I could have a piece of pie," went on the little girl. "I think you bake the loveliest pies, Dinah! Honest I do!"

"Yes'm, honey lamb, dey is good!" admitted the cook, with pardonable pride in her work. "But Ah cain't cut a fresh pie fo' yo!"

"Oh, dear!" sighed Flossie.

There was a noise on the cellar stairs and Dinah wondered if Freddie were coming up.

But nothing like this happened. The cellar door did not open, and Flossie did not appear to have heard the noise.

"Isn't there anything you can give me to eat, Dinah?" she asked wistfully. "I'm so hungry!"

"Bress yo' heart, honey lamb! Ah kin gib yo' some 'lasses cookies!" replied Dinah.

"Oh, molasses cookies! I just love them!" cried Flossie, and when she had several in her hands she ran out, crying: "Freddie! Freddie! Where are you? I got cookies!"

Freddie did not answer, and the voice of Flossie died away as she ran in search of him.

But pretty soon the kitchen cellar door opened and Freddie's head was thrust out. Dinah heard the noise of the knob and turned to look at the little fellow.

"Is she gone?" whispered Freddie. "Is Flossie gone?"

"She suah has," was the reply.

"I'm glad she didn't see me," he went on. "I got it hid down behind the coal bin."

"Good lan'!" exclaimed Dinah. "Whut's it all about, anyhow?"

"Hush!" begged Freddie in a whisper. "I got Daddy a present for his birthday—it's to-morrow, you know. I found a basket and

I picked it full of flowers. And in the bottom of the basket is a new baseball. I saved up my money and bought it for him. He'll think there's only flowers in the basket, but down under them's the baseball. An' if Daddy doesn't want it to play with himself he can give it to me; can't he, Dinah?"

"Ah reckon he can, honey!" chuckled the colored cook.

"Don't you think that's a 'riginal present for Daddy, Dinah?" asked the little fellow. "I wanted to give him something 'riginal!"

"It suah am 'riginal, all right," admitted Dinah. "An' here's some cookies fo' yo'. Better run out now an' play!"

"I will," agreed Freddie. "But don't tell anybody about my 'riginal present for Daddy, will you?"

"No, Ah won't," Dinah promised.

It was a little while after this that Flossie came running back, begging for more cookies.

"Have yo' done eat all dem up I gib yo'?" asked Dinah.

"I gave some to Mary Blake and some to Sallie Porter," explained Flossie, naming two of her playmates. "So I didn't have many myself."

"Dat's too bad!" murmured Dinah. "But dere's plenty mo' cookies! He'p yo'se'f, honey," and she brought out the pan.

Flossie looked around the kitchen to make sure none but Dinah could hear her, and then she whispered:

"Dinah, do you know what was in that box I hid in the stair closet? Do you?"

The cook could pretty well guess by this time, but she pretended she did not know and shook her head.

"It's a present for daddy's birthday," went on Flossie. "I'm going to give it to him when we eat supper. Do you know what it is?"

Again Dinah shook her head.

"Well, I'll tell you, but you mustn't tell anybody!" whispered Flossie. "It's a little folding go-cart for a doll. I think Daddy will like that, don't you? It's the cutest little go-cart and it all folds up small and goes in a box. But you can unfold it big enough to ride my largest doll. Isn't that a nice present for Daddy?"

"It suah am!" laughed Dinah.

Though Bert and Nan said nothing to her about the packages they had so secretly hidden, Dinah guessed that the older twins had also bought presents for their father's birthday, which occurred on the morrow, but which would be celebrated that evening, as usual.

"Ah wonders if Bert an' Nan got t'ings laik Freddie an' Flossie?" chuckled Dinah. "Dose small twins suah am lookin' out for derse'ves!"

It was later in the afternoon, and the Bobbsey twins were gathering about the house to get washed and dressed for supper, when the doorbell rang.

"I'll go!" cried Nan, making a dash for the hall.

Bert was also ready to answer the ring, but his twin sister was a little bit ahead of him. And Flossie and Freddie were not far behind Bert, who ran out into the front hall in time to see Nan talking to the driver of an express wagon.

"Does Mr. Richard Bobbsey live here?" asked the expressman.

"Yes, sir," answered Nan.

"But he isn't home from the office yet," added Bert.

"Well, I guess that won't matter," went

on the man, with a laugh. "I have a box here for him. The charges are paid so I will leave it, if one of you will sign the receipt for it."

"I'll sign," offered Nan, as she had often heard her mother say.

The box was set down in the front hall. It was of wood, and seemed quite heavy.

"What's in it?" asked Bert.

"I don't know," the expressman answered. "Maybe it has a fortune in gold in it. Anyhow, there's something that rattles. And a letter came to the office, asking us to deliver the box just before supper this evening. Maybe it has something good to eat in it."

He drove away with a laugh, while the Bobbsey twins gathered about the mysterious box in the hall—a box that had come to their father on the eve of his birthday.

What was in it?

That is what each of the Bobbsey twins wondered.

CHAPTER II

QUEER NOISES

"WHAT is going on down there, my dears?" called Mrs. Bobbsey from the top of the stairs. Down in the hall below she could see, gathered about the mysterious box, the four twins. She had heard the bell ring, and at first thought it was her husband, coming home early on account of the birthday celebration.

But when she heard the strange tones of the expressman she realized that something else had happened, and she was curious to know what it was about.

"It's a big box for Daddy," explained Bert.

"We don't know where it's from," went on Nan.

"And the 'spress man didn't know what was in it," added Flossie.

"But I guess it's for Daddy's birthday," exclaimed Freddie. "And I got——"

He stopped just in time. He had been about to speak of the "'riginal" present he himself had hidden down cellar.

"Well, if it's for Daddy we must let it alone until he comes home," said Mrs. Bobbsey. "Come now and get ready for supper. It will not be long before Daddy arrives, and he will open the box."

"I wonder what's in it," murmured Bert as he moved away, with a backward look at the mysterious package.

"And I wonder where it's from," said Nan, who was as curious as her brother.

But they would not think of trying to open it, or of trying to pry off one corner to look inside. Indeed, this would have been hard to do, since the box was strongly made.

Flossie and Freddie were as eager as their older brother and sister to know about the box. But perhaps they were thinking so much of their own presents that they did not say much about the package the expressman had delivered.

While the four are getting ready for the evening meal I will beg just a few moments of the time of my new readers to introduce them to the Bobbsey twins. There were four of the twins, as you have learned by this time. Bert and Nan, who had dark hair and eyes, were the older pair, and Flossie and Freddie, whose eyes were blue and whose hair was golden, came next. Their father was Richard Bobbsey, who owned a large lumberyard in the eastern city of Lakeport on Lake Metoka.

"The Bobbsey Twins" is the name of the first book which tells about these children and what happened to them and their friends. After that Bert and his brother and sisters had many adventures in the country, at the seashore, and at school.

From Snow Lodge the twins went on a voyage in a houseboat and then to Meadow Brook. Happenings at home, in a great city, on Blueberry Island and, later, on the deep, blue sea, kept the boys and girls busy for several vacations, and then they went to Washington, where some strange happenings occurred. But no more strange, perhaps, than in the great West or at Cedar Camp.

The county fair, where Mr. Bobbsey took his children, was a most interesting event, and when they went camping out they had great fun.

But the finding of Baby May was, perhaps,

the most mysterious thing that ever happened to the Bobbseys. They found a little baby on their doorstep after a storm, and kept the infant, calling her Baby May Washington Bobbsey, because a queer woman, who had been seen at the railroad station with the baby's basket, had murmured a name something like "Washington."

But this proveh to be a mistake, since the baby's right name was Jenny Watson. She was the daughter of Mr. and Mrs. Henry Watson, and had been left in charge of a Mrs. Martin while Mr. and Mrs. Watson made a voyage to South America. Mrs. Martin was Mrs. Watson's cousin.

Because of an accident, when some dishes fell on her head, Mrs. Martin went crazy and had an idea that she must give Baby Jenny away, which she did, by leaving the infant on the Bobbsey steps.

In due time "Baby May," the name by which Flossie and Freddie still called the little child, was taken to her mother and father, and Mrs. Martin, who recovered from her crazy spell, and the Watsons became good friends of the Bobbsey family.

Following the excitement over the finding

of the baby, the Bobbsey twins had some very strange adventures which you will find set down in the book just before the one you are now reading. That volume is entitled "The Bobbsey Twins Keeping House," and tells what happened when Mr. and Mrs. Bobbsey had to go away, when Dinah and Sam also departed, and when Mrs. Pry, the housekeeper who had been engaged by Mrs. Bobbsey, was taken ill.

However, everything comes to an end in time, and finally all was straightened out in the Bobbsey house. This took place in the winter, and now it was the beginning of summer, and the eve of Mr. Bobbsey's birthday.

The mysterious box—at least the twins thought it was mysterious—had arrived, and they were all excited, waiting for their father to come home to open it.

"Isn't Daddy late to-night?" asked Nan, when she had finished dressing and had gone into her mother's room.

"No, not later than usual," answered Mrs. Bobbsey, with a smile as she glanced at the clock on her bureau.

"Then time is going awfully slow!" commented Bert, looking in from the hall. "I wish Daddy would hurry! I want to see him open his birthday box."

"Don't be too sure that is a box for Daddy's birthday," remarked Mrs. Bobbsey. "It may be something about business."

"If it was business they would send it to him at his office," came from Nan.

"Besides," added Bert, "the expressman said they got a letter asking 'em to deliver the box before supper this evening, and everybody knows we always give Daddy his presents at supper on the night before his birthday."

"So we do," agreed Mrs. Bobbsey. "But not every one knows that, Bert. However, if you children have any presents for your father perhaps you had better be getting them ready. I suppose you are going to give him something, aren't you?" she asked, with a smile.

Instead of answering, the four twins looked one at the other. Each one was trying to keep a secret, but it was not easy. But before they could reply there was heard from the hall below the noise of a door opening.

"There's Daddy now!" cried Bert.

"Wait for me!" begged Flossie, as she saw the others make a dash out of the room.

"Let me go first!" begged Freddie, and he was so anxious to get ahead of Bert that he stooped down and crawled between the legs of his brother, just as Bert was in the doorway of his mother's room.

So eager was Freddie, and such a shove did he give himself to crawl through Bert's legs that, before he knew what was happening, the fat little lad had slipped, rolled to the top of the stairs, and then he rolled all the way down, bumping from step to step.

But, as it happened, Mr. Bobbsey reached the bottom of the flight of stairs in time to catch Freddie before the little fellow reached the last step.

"Well, well, what's all this?" cried Mr. Bobbsey, holding Freddie in his arms. "Is my little fireman trying to make a rescue?" Mr. Bobbsey often spoke of Freddie as a "fireman," since the little fellow was so fond of playing that game. He had a toy fire engine that spouted real water, too. And Flossie's pet name was "little fat fairy."

"Is he hurt?" asked Mrs. Bobbsey, coming down the stairs.

"No—I'm all right!" protested Freddie. "I—now—I just slipped—that's all. I was in a hurry."

"I should say you were!" laughed his father. "But you are so fat and the stairs are so thickly carpeted, that you aren't hurt a bit!"

Freddie was set upon his feet, and, with the others, made a circle about Mr. Bobbsey and the mysterious box. Then, for the first time, the lumber merchant appeared aware of the bulky package in the lower hall.

"What's this?" he asked.

"Something for you, it seems," answered his wife.

"It's for your birthday!" cried Nan.

"It came by express!" added Bert.

"And we'd like to see what's in it," remarked Flossie.

"Don't go 'way now," begged Freddie. "'Cause there's other things for you—I mean for your birthday—I guess they are," he added, not wanting to appear too sure. "But open this box first."

"All right," agreed Mr. Bobbsey. "It's a

surprise to me, I'll say that. I don't even know where it's from."

"Maybe it tells on the other side," suggested Bert, who had brought a hammer and a screw driver for his father to use in opening the box.

"Perhaps," was the answer. "We'll take a look."

As he turned the box on its other side to discover whence it had come, a strange sound was heard issuing from inside.

"Oh!" cried Flossie. "It sounds like a little baby!"

"Nonsense!" laughed her mother. "There would be no baby in such a box!"

Mr. Bobbsey now had the box turned on the other side, and there appeared a card which read:

"From Mr. and Mrs. Henry Watson of Cloverbank!"

"Oh, Mr. Watson remembered your birthday! How nice!" exclaimed Mrs. Bobbsey. "I didn't think he knew it."

"Nor did I," said Mr. Bobbsey, as he got ready to pry off the box cover.

"Watson! Watson!" murmured Bert, thinking hard. "Oh, yes!" he cried. "That's the name of the father and mother of Baby May, whom we found on our doorstep. That box came from Baby May!"

"Yes, or from her parents," said Mr. Bobbsey.

As he moved the box, in order to get a better chance to pry off the cover, again there came from inside it a strange wailing cry.

"Oh, Daddy! Open it—quick!" cried Freddie. "Baby May must be inside that box. Her father and mother sent her back to you for a birthday present! Open it— quick—and take Baby May out!"

"Nonsense!" exclaimed Mrs. Bobbsey. "Nobody would put a baby in a box like that and send it by express!"

The queer noises sounded again, and, really, they seemed to be such cries as a baby might make.

"Open the box! Open the box!" cried Nan, much excited, and Mr. Bobbsey hurriedly began using the hammer and screw driver while the twins and their mother leaned eagerly forward.

CHAPTER III

AN INVITATION

NEITHER Mr. nor Mrs. Bobbsey thought for a moment that "Baby May," as they still called her, was in the box. Still there was certainly something very queer about the noises that came from the express package.

"It sure is a baby," murmured Flossie.

"It's a queer baby then," declared Nan. "I can see a lot of green and red and yellow things, and no baby is that color!"

For by this time her father had removed some of the boards from the box and a view could be had inside. And, as Nan had said, there was a glimpse of something red, green, and yellow.

"Maybe Baby May—I mean Baby Jenny —has paint on," suggested Flossie.

"Ho! Ho!" laughed Freddie. "Who ever heard of painting a baby?"

"My doll has paint on, and she's a baby," retorted Flossie. Then the little girl thought of the present she had bought for her father— the folding go-cart hidden in the closet under the stairs, and she cried: "Oh, do please hurry, Daddy! Open your present and then maybe you'll get some other presents!"

"Oh, I hardly think so," replied Mr. Bobbsey, still working away with the hammer and the screw driver. "I guess this is the only present I'll get this birthday. It was very kind of Mr. Watson to remember me!"

Though he said this, Mr. Bobbsey did not really mean that, for well he knew each of the twins, as well as his wife, would give him something. They had every year since the two older twins were big enough to know about birthdays.

But Flossie and Freddie, thinking their father really meant what he said, burst out eagerly to deny his fear that he was to be forgotten.

"Oh, no, Daddy!" cried Flossie. "You're going to get another present—a lovely one!"

"Yes, and another one too, besides that!" added Freddie.

" You don't mean it!" cried Mr. Bobbsey, pretending to be very much surprised. "Well! Well! I must hurry and finish opening this box, for, after I see what is in it, I'll get the other presents—maybe."

"You sure will!" chuckled Bert.

"Listen!" whispered Nan.

Again came a low, wailing cry from within the box.

"There!" suddenly cried Mr. Bobbsey. He pried off nearly all of the top boards and out from the midst of a lot of vegetables jumped—Snoop! Snoop, the big, black Bobbsey cat!

"Oh!" cried Freddie. "Look at him!"

"Snoop!" shouted Bert.

"How in the world did he get in there?" asked Nan.

But Snoop waved his tail, rubbed up against the legs of fat little Flossie, and gave voice to a miaowing cry.

"There!" exclaimed Mrs. Bobbsey. "It was Snoop who was crying like a baby. He was shut up inside that box, and his voice sounded muffled, as if he were down in the cellar. That's what made it seem to be a baby's cry."

"But how did Snoop get in the box?" asked Freddie.

Mr. Bobbsey turned the express package over on its side and then it was seen how Snoop had gotten inside. One of the bottom boards was broken. There was a hole large enough for the black cat to have crawled inside, and as Snoop was very like his name, always snooping around in strange places, that is what he had done. He had crawled in through the hole and had curled up among a lot of vegetables. Then, when the box was turned over, so Mr. Bobbsey could read the card, telling whence it had come, Snoop could not get out. So he had cried mournfully to be released.

"Oh, it's a lot of vegetables and berries in the box!" said Nan, as she took a look, after Snoop had jumped out and the mystery of the "baby's" cries had been solved.

"Yes, it's quite a load of farm and garden produce," said Mr. Bobbsey. "Mr. Watson must have a large place at Cloverbank. Here's a note," and he picked up one that was stuck in a bunch of beets.

The note was from Mr. Watson. It contained only a few short lines, saying:

"Dear Mr. Bobbsey: My wife and I remembered that this was your birthday, so we send you some of our early vegetables and some berries. You were so kind to Baby Jenny that we shall never forget you. You will hear from me again very soon."

"How kind of him!" murmured Mrs. Bobbsey.

"Did Baby May—I mean Baby Jenny— write a letter?" asked Freddie.

"No, she is hardly old enough," answered his mother, while Mr. Bobbsey began lifting out the bunches of early vegetables and the boxes of berries. It was the green, red, and yellow color of the fruits and vegetables which the children had glimpsed through cracks in the box. So quickly had the farm and garden produce come by express that they were very fresh and good.

"I guess we'll not have any of these for supper," announced Mr. Bobbsey, as he reached down and rubbed Snoop, who was now purring happily since he was out of the prison into which he had crawled. "And, speaking of supper, I am ready to eat mine."

"We're going to have pie," declared Bert.

"I saw Dinah baking them, and I guess she made some extra ones on account of your birthday, Daddy."

"Did she? That's nice!" laughed Mr. Bobbsey. "You must have been in the kitchen to find out about the pies, Bert."

"Yes, sir, I was," admitted Bert, with a quick look at Nan. But she seemed to be thinking of something else.

"Come now, children, we will eat and then we'll unpack the vegetables from Cloverbank," suggested Mrs. Bobbsey. "What a pretty name for a place," she went on. "It must be a delightful country up there."

"I wish we could go to the country again," said Bert. "School will soon be over and we'll have a long vacation."

"Where are we going this vacation?" asked Nan.

"We haven't decided yet," answered her mother. "But come—we shall be late for supper unless we hurry, and that makes more work for Dinah!"

She led the way to the dining room, with Flossie and Freddie whispering on the way:

"When can we give Daddy his presents?"

"You might as well get them now, I suppose," said Mrs. Bobbsey, with a laugh as she glanced at her husband. "There will be no peace at the table until you do, and you won't eat anything until this excitement is over. Get the presents now!"

"Whoopee!" yelled Bert, who was almost as excited as were the smaller twins.

"Mine's in the cellar!" cried Freddie, as he made a dash for the kitchen.

"Be careful going down the stairs!" warned his mother.

"Mine's upstairs," remarked Nan.

"So's mine!" added Bert, with a quick look at her. "I didn't see you up there hiding it, though," he went on.

"And I didn't see you," laughed Nan. "I came in through the kitchen."

"So'd I!" cried Bert, with a chuckle.

"I did, too!" added Flossie. "And my present's under the front stairs in the little dark closet. Don't you look until I get it for you, Daddy!" she warned. "Don't peek, will you?"

"All right, I won't!" promised Mr. Bobbsey. "See, my eyes are tight shut—you'll have to lead me to the table, Mother," he went on to his wife.

"Oh, isn't this fun!" laughed Flossie, as the children scattered to get the birthday presents from the various hiding places.

"Well, whut's gwine on now?" demanded Dinah, as she saw Freddie dash through the kitchen and down the cellar stairs.

"It's time for the secret!" he breathlessly explained.

"Well, Ah suah am glad ob dat!" chuckled the colored cook. "Mah nice supper am 'bout ruined wif all dis delay!"

They were soon all gathered about the table, Mr. Bobbsey still with his eyes tightly shut. One after the other, the twins walked up and put their presents in front of him. Not until all four packages were there did Mrs. Bobbsey call:

"Ready! Open your eyes!"

When he opened them and saw the packages, Mr. Bobbsey pretended that he had suddenly awakened, and was still dreaming. He rubbed his eyes and said:

"There must be some mistake!"

"What mistake, Daddy?" asked Nan.

"Why, all these presents!" was the answer. "I have only *one* birthday, but there are *four* presents! I'd better send three of them back!"

"No! No!"

"They're all for you!"

"Every one!"

"They're all yours—all four!"

Thus cried the Bobbsey twins in joyous excitement. Of course Mr. Bobbsey knew that all the while; but he did love to tease the twins. Then he took up first the big bundle which Freddie had hidden down in the cellar.

"Oh, what lovely flowers!" cried the birthday man. "Oh, how I love flowers!" and he buried his nose in them.

"I picked 'em—every one!" cried Freddie, in great delight. "And there's something else in there, too, Daddy! Down in the bottom! Look!"

"Well, I declare. A baseball! Of all things!" exclaimed Mr. Bobbsey as he took it out. "That's just what I've been wanting —a baseball so I could have a little game at noon with the men in the lumberyard. It's a fine ball, too—and such a bouncer!" he went on, as he threw it to the floor and caught it as it rebounded.

"And if you don't want it—or if you get tired of it," said Freddie, "why, you can give it to me. Sammie Shull and I are going to get up a basball nine."

"All right," his father said. "If I find it's too small for me and the men—and it looks as if it might be too small—you may take it, Freddie."

"Yes—that's what I thought," said the lad, while his father and mother smiled at each other.

"That's my present to you," said Flossie, pointing to the square box she had hidden in the stair closet. "I hope you'll like it."

Mr. Bobbsey took out the folding doll go-cart. First there was a puzzled look on his face. Then he smiled as he cried:

"Oh, I see, this is a new kind of necktie!"

"No, it isn't!" protested Flossie.

"Then it must be an umbrella to keep off the rain," went on the lumber merchant, pretending to be puzzled about the folding go-cart, though, all the while, he knew what it was.

"Oh, no, Daddy! 'Tisn't an umbrella!" cried Flossie. "It's a little carriage for my doll. You unfold it and bend out the wheels.

Then, when you take me for a walk and I get
tired of carrying my doll, you can put it in
the go-cart and wheel her for me. I think
that's a nice present for you—isn't it.
Daddy?"

"It's the most beautiful present I ever
got!" declared her father, with a laugh, "and
I'm going to give you a kiss for it. I must
also kiss Freddie for the baseball. That was
a fine present, too! That is, unless my little
fireman is too big to be kissed?" and Mr.
Bobbsey looked at Freddie a moment after he
had kissed Flossie.

"I don't mind being kissed—on your birthday," said the little fellow. "But not much
at other times. I'm getting too big for it."

"So you are," said Mr. Bobbsey, with a
laugh. "Well, bring in your doll, Flossie,
and let's see how she fits my new folding
birthday go-cart," and again Mr. and Mrs.
Bobbsey laughed at each other.

The doll had been put in and wheeled
about. But there were still two packages to
be opened—those which Nan and Bert had
put beside their father's plate.

These gifts were not quite as " 'riginal" as
those Flossie and Freddie had bought, for

the older twins had asked their mother what she thought their father would like. With the help of her mother Nan had bought Mr. Bobbsey a bathrobe which, he said, was just what he had long needed. Bert's present was a golf sweater which, his father stated, was just the color he had long been hoping to get.

"This is the best birthday I ever remember!" declared Mr. Bobbsey, when his wife had presented him with a new wallet in which to carry his money, cards, and papers. "What with the flowers, the baseball, the go-cart, the robe, the sweater, the wallet, and the box of fruits and vegetables from Cloverbank—why, I never got so many things before!"

It was a jolly birthday celebration, and the children talked of little else while the meal was going on. Presently Nan turned the conversation another way by asking:

"What do you suppose Mr. Watson meant by saying you would soon hear from him again, Daddy?"

"I don't know, my dear, unless he meant that he would write now and again to let us hear how the baby was getting along," was the answer. "You know, we grew very fond of Baby May, as we called her, and your mother and I did not want to give her up, though of course we had to. I think Mr. Watson must mean he is going to write again to tell us about Baby Jenny, as we must learn to call her."

But a letter came from Cloverbank before any of the Bobbseys thought it possible to receive one. Just as supper was finished there came a ring at the doorbell, and Flossie cried:

"Oh, maybe it's more presents for Daddy's birthday."

Instead of an expressman, however, it proved to be a boy from the post-office with a special delivery letter. These letters come at any time of the day or night, after the regular mail is delivered.

"A special delivery!" murmured Mrs. Bobbsey, as she saw the blue stamp with the picture on it of a messenger boy running. "I wonder who it is from?"

"It's easy to tell that even without opening it," said Mr. Bobbsey. "It's from Henry Watson of Cloverbank. His name is on the envelope."

"Oh, he said you'd hear from him again

soon, and you have!" cried Nan. "Do open it, Daddy, and see what it's about."

When Mr. Bobbsey read the letter a smile came to his face.

"Well, this seems to settle the summer vacation problem for us, Mother!" he exclaimed. "This is an invitation from Mr. and Mrs. Watson and also from Baby May—I mean Baby Jenny—to come and spend the summer with them at Cloverbank. Among other things, Mr. Watson writes:

"'Can't you and the children visit us? Baby "May" would surely love to see the Bobbsey twins.'"

"Oh, can we go?" chorused the Bobbsey twins.

But before either Mr. or Mrs. Bobbsey could answer there sounded a loud crash out in the kitchen, and the voice of Dinah cried:

"Dar! Now luck whut yo' all done! Mah goodness!"

CHAPTER IV

THE PRIZE OFFER

SILENCE followed the crash and the excited call of Dinah. Mrs. Bobbsey thought something serious might have happened, and she said to her husband:

"Perhaps you had better go to see what it is."

That it was nothing serious was made plain a moment later, even before Mr. Bobbsey reached the place, for Dinah could be heard laughing, and between her chuckles came the voice of Sam Johnson, her husband, complaining:

"Git offen me now! Does yo' heah? Git offen mah haid! Mah good lan', such goin's on as dere am heah! Git off, Ah tells yo'!"

When the Bobbseys entered the kitchen they saw Sam dancing around and trying to reach something on his head. This something proved to be Snoop, the big black cat, who was clinging with his claws to Sam's thick, kinky, black, woolly hair.

"Snoop suah does know when he's got a soft place!" chuckled Dinah, who was laughing so hard that she could not go to the aid of her husband.

"Take him offen me! Take him off, Ah tells yo'!" begged Sam, dancing about the kitchen.

"I'll get him," offered Nan, who had trained Snoop to do a few tricks. "Stand still, Sam," begged the little girl, "and I'll get Snoop off for you! How'd he get on your head?"

"He done jumped there—dat's how he got," explained Sam, with a rueful face as he did what Nan advised and remained in one spot. Then the little girl brought a chair over close to the colored man-of-all-work, and, climbing up, lifted Snoop down. As soon as the cat felt himself in the hands of Nan, the animal released his claws from their firm hold in Sam's wool. It was this grip of the cat's claws that had prevented Sam himself from lifting Snoop down. The more he pulled on the animal the tighter Snoop clung, for he was afraid of falling.

"What happened, Dinah?" asked Mrs. Bobbsey, who, with her husband, stood in the kitchen doorway, laughing at Sam's rueful face.

"Oh, I guess dat cat Snoop mus' 'a' had a birfday himse'f," explained Dinah. "He's dat smart an' libely he mus' feel laik he's about one yeah old—jumpin' 'round laik he was."

"What did he do?" asked Bert.

"Oh, he jump up on a chair when I wasn't lookin'!" went on Dinah. "An' his tail knock a dish offen de table an' bruk it— bruk de dish Ah means. Den I grabbed up de broom to make a swoop at Snoop an' just den Sam come in an' I hit him 'stid ob hittin' de cat. An' dat scared Snoop, I guess, 'cause he make a jump an' he git right up on top ob de do' and den—den——"

But Dinah was laughing so heartily at the recollection of what had happened that she could not go on with the story. So Sam continued it by adding:

"Dat cat he jes' jump right down offen de

do' right on top ob mah haid, an' dar he stuck laik a chestnut burr! Golly, but he suah did stick his claws in mah ha'r!" and then Sam chuckled.

"Well, I'm glad it was no worse," remarked Mrs. Bobbsey, with a smile. "One broken dish doesn't matter, especially on a birthday. But perhaps you had better take Snoop out, Nan, so he won't make any more trouble for Dinah."

"I'll give him a ride in Flossie's doll's go-cart that she got for Daddy!" laughed Nan.

"No, you will not!" protested the other Bobbsey girl. "I'm going to give my doll a ride. Come on, Daddy," she begged. "Let's take a walk and ride my doll."

"And let's have a catch with my ball—I mean the ball I gave you!" cried Freddie.

"Maybe I'd better put on my new robe and wear my new birthday sweater before I go doll-carriaging and ball-playing," suggested Mr. Bobbsey, with a laugh.

"Well, don't take the new wallet I gave you," warned his wife. "I put a penny in, for luck, and you might lose it."

But after again admiring the robe and the sweater, the gifts of Bert and Nan. Mr.

Bobbsey laid them aside and had a few catches with Freddie, using the new ball. Then he wheeled Flossie's folding go-cart giving the little girl's best doll a ride.

After that the four twins went off by themselves to play with some of their boy and girl chums in the twilight of the fading June day, while Mr. and Mrs. Bobbsey sat on the porch.

"Do you really think?" asked Mrs. Bobbsey of her husband, "that you will take the children to Cloverbank for the summer?"

"I don't know," he answered. "What do you think? Mr. Watson seems to want to have us come. I know he has a large place there with plenty of room in the house, and there is a big farm, an orchard, and woods near by where the twins could play. There is also a creek and a little lake, I believe."

"It sounds like a wonderful place to spend the summer," responded his wife. "And we always go somewhere. Just where is Cloverbank?"

"It is outside the town of Hitchville," was the answer. "It's about a day's ride in the automobile. We could get there without much trouble."

"Well, if you think they really want us,

suppose you write and tell Mr. Watson if he will take the whole family for the summer we'll be glad to come," suggested Mrs. Bobbsey.

"I know the children will like it," remarked their father.

Twilight faded into darkness and, tired with their evening of play, the Bobbsey twins came slowly back home. Soon Flossie and Freddie were undressed and in bed, with Bert and Nan getting ready to follow them a little later. But first the two older twins wanted to know more about the plans for the summer.

"We have about decided to go to Cloverbank," said Mrs. Bobbsey.

"Oh, goodie!" exclaimed Nan. "Then I can take out Baby May—I mean Baby Jenny."

"I hope there's a place where I can swim and catch fish," murmured Bert.

"Are you going to swim after the fish and catch them?" asked Nan, with a laugh.

"Oh, you know what I mean," he answered. "I can't do both at the same time, of course. Though once, when Danny Rugg and I were in swimming, a fish brushed its tail against my legs and I almost caught it, only I wasn't quick enough."

"I think there will be plenty of swimming, fishing, and other fun at Mr. Watson's Cloverbank place," said Mr. Bobbsey. "And now I think you and Nan had better see which of you will be first asleep," he went on, for it was getting late. Supper had been delayed longer than usual because of the birthday celebration, and the children had been allowed to stay up a little later than was customary.

"Oh, won't we have fun in Cloverbank!" whispered Nan to her brother, as they went up the stairs.

"I just guess we will!" he answered. "I can hardly wait for the time to come!"

"Me either. Good-night!"

"Good-night!" answered Bert, as he went softly into the room where he slept with Freddie. Nan slept with Flossie. Both the small twins were sound asleep. So were Bert and Nan a little later.

School had not yet closed for the summer. There was about another week of classes before the long vacation. And the morning after their father's birthday the Bobbsey twins started for the schoolhouse soon after the first bell began ringing.

"Hello, Danny!" called Bert when he saw the Rugg boy coming up the street. "Don't you wish you had another snowball to break a church window with?" and Bert laughed as he recalled what had happened in the winter, when Danny had broken a stained-glass window and had blamed Bert for it. But the truth had come out, through the loss of Danny's gold ring, and Danny had begged Bert's pardon, so the boys were good friends once more.

"Yes, a pile of snow would feel good just about now," agreed Danny. "It sure is a not day! I'll be glad when school closes."

"So'll I," assented Bert. "Where you going this summer?"

"Down to the seashore, I guess," Danny answered.

"We're going to the country," went on Bert. "To a place called Cloverbank. It's near Hitchville."

"Oh, that's a swell place!" cried Danny. "I know a fellow who went there. There's dandy fishing in the creek!"

"I'm glad of it," said Bert. Then the

boys and girls passed into the schoolhouse.
I cannot say that any one was much interested
in lessons that day. It was too hot to study
much. Realizing this, the teacher in the
room where Bert and Nan sat had an idea.
She was trying to get the children to write a
"composition," which, as most of you know,
isn't easy work.

"You children will find it much easier to
write compositions," Miss Skell said, "if
you will take as subjects something you know
about. Instead of trying to write about the
stars, as some of you did last week, try to
write about something on earth. You don't
know much about the stars—no one does.
But you may know a great deal about a nest
that some birds have built in your apple tree.
So write about those birds."

"And while I am talking about compositions," the teacher went on, "I want to say
that I am going to offer a prize to the boy or
girl who, during the vacation, will write the
best story, or composition, about something
that happens to him or her this summer.
Write about something real, in the best way
you can, and bring the story back to school
when it opens again in the fall.

"The best compositions will be read before the class, and I will decide who is to get the prize, which will be a set of books. The winner may choose the books from a list I will have on my desk."

Murmurs of delight and surprise were heard about the room. This was something new— a prize for a summer composition! At once the children, who had been dull and listless because of the heat, seemed bright and cheerful. Miss Skell smiled at the success of her plan.

"Now we will have some practice work in writing compositions," she went on. "You will be better able to do the work this summer when there is no school if you practice a bit now. So we will begin!"

Every boy and girl was most eager now, especially Nan Bobbsey. She was always good at composition work—perhaps not the best in the room, but certainly better than Bert, though he tried. But, really, Bert cared more about playing games than about writing compositions.

"Oh, if I could only win that prize!" thought Nan. "It would be wonderful! I wonder what I can find to write about? Perhaps something may happen while we are at Cloverbank."

Danny Rugg raised his hand, indicating that he wanted to ask a question.

"What is it, Danny?" inquired the teacher.

"How long must the composition be?" the boy asked. "I mean how many pages?"

"Oh, as many as you like," was the reply. "But it must not be too short!" went on Miss Skell quickly. "I want more than a few sentences. Try to make a story about what happens to you this summer—a story such as you might read in a book. Who knows—perhaps some of you, when you grow up, may write books. I hope you will."

"I'd love to write a book!" murmured Nan to Nellie Parks, who sat with her.

"I'd rather read books than write them," whispered Nellie.

"Quiet now, children, if you please," suggested Miss Skell, for she had allowed a little whispering following her announcement of the prize offer. "Now we will begin our composition work. You may each write me a short one on the subject of what happened to you yesterday after school—in the afternoon, evening, or night!"

Just as Bert Bobbsey was settling himself to his task, the door opened and a girl from one of the higher classes entered with a note which she gave to Miss Skell. The teacher read it quickly, and then said in a low voice:

"Mr. Tarton wants to see you in his office, Bert."

What could this mean? Mr. Tarton was the principal of the school. Usually it was not very pleasant to have to go to his office.

Bert slowly left his seat. He, too, was wondering what could have happened.

CHAPTER V

OFF FOR CLOVERBANK

NAN BOBBSEY and some of her girl chums, as well as Danny Rugg and the boys with whom Bert Bobbsey played, also wondered why Bert had to go to the principal's office.

"Did Bert do anything?" whispered Grace Lavine, who sat behind Nan.

"I don't know," was the low-voiced reply. "I don't think so. I didn't see him."

"Well, anyhow, he couldn't have thrown any snowballs," said Nellie Parks. "I mean like the time he once did and Danny said he broke the church window."

"No," agreed Nan, remembering the winter when she and her brother and the smaller twins "kept house," with Mrs. Pry ill in bed.

"Was Bert fighting with any of the fellows?" inquired Charlie Mason of Danny, who sat near him. "Mr. Tarton doesn't like fighting."

"I know he doesn't," Danny answered. "But I don't believe Bert was. It must be for something else."

"Attend to your lessons now, children. Bert will be back soon," said Miss Skell.

Nan gave a sigh of relief on hearing this. It could not be so very serious, then.

As for Bert, his heart was beating rather faster than usual as he entered Mr. Tarton's office, but the smile with which the head of the school greeted the pupil seemed to tell the boy that he was not brought down for anything serious.

"Good-morning, Bert!" said the principal. "I called you here to see if you have a top in your pocket—you know what I mean—a top that spins with a string wound around it. Have you such a top?"

"Why—er—yes—yes, sir," stammered the boy. What in the world could Mr. Tarton want of a top? Could he have turned childish and have a desire to play with a top in his office, Bert wondered.

Then another thought came into the mind of the lad. Perhaps Mr. Tarton thought Bert had been playing with a top during class time. So the boy said:

"But I didn't have it out in the room, Mr. Tarton! Really I didn't! I was spinning it in front of the school, but I put it in my pocket when I came in and——"

"Yes, I know you did, Bert," and again Mr. Tarton smiled. "I saw you spinning your top, and that's why I sent for you. I want you to come and spin the top for me in front of the class in science."

This was more and more puzzling.

The principal must have seen that Burt was puzzled and a bit worried, for he laughed a little and said:

"It's all right, Bert. The science class is studying motion, and I want to illustrate to them the principle of the gyroscope. I have that kind of a top here, but I had no common top, and I remembered seeing you spin yours, and that it was a large red one, which can easily be seen when you spin it on the platform in front of the high-school class. You see I want to show the science boys and girls the difference between a gyroscope top and the common top."

"And you want me to spin a top in school—for a lesson?" asked Bert in surprise.

"That's it—yes," answered the principal.

"I think you know what a gyroscope top is, don't you?" Bert did, having been given one for Christmas. Mr. Tarton quickly brought his queer top out and spun it.

A gyroscope top is a heavy, small wheel fitted inside a round ring of metal, and the ring has a sort of top peg on it. When the heavy wheel inside the metal ring is set spinning by means of a string wound about it and pulled off, the wheel goes so fast that it will hold up the metal ring in any position. Thus the gyroscope top will spin upside down, lying on its side and in many other positions.

"But your top will spin in one way only, and that is standing straight up, Bert," said the principal. "That's what I want the boys and girls in the high-school class to understand. Of course I could tell them about it, but they will learn much more quickly if they see the two different tops spinning in front of them. So come with me now, if you please, and bring your top."

Bert could hardly help smiling as he followed the principal to the high-school part of the building. It seemed so queer to be asked, as a favor, to spin a top in class. But the older boys and girls were as much in earnest as was Mr. Tarton. They wanted to learn this rule about spinning bodies, for the earth we live on, you know, spins about like a giant top. So the high-school lads and lassies did not laugh when Mr. Tarton wound up and spun the gyroscope nor when Bert set his red top to spinning. They asked many questions and seemed eager to learn. Bert himself was much interested.

"You are a good top-spinner," said Mr. Tarton to him when the lesson was over. "You may go back to your class, and you may take the gyroscope top with you and tell Miss Skell I said you could spin it and show the smaller boys and girls how it works."

So the mystery of why Bert was sent to the principal's office was soon solved. Going back to his room, in a few words Bert told Miss Skell about it. He also delivered the message about the gyroscope, and soon the boys and girls were much interested in watching Bert spin it on Miss Skell's desk.

"If she'd let us write a composition about that funny top I believe I could do a good one," said Nellie Parks to Nan when the class was let out for the noon recess.

"But the prize composition must be about something that happens on our summer vacation," answered Nan. "Oh, I do hope I win the prize!"

"I hope you do, too," said Nellie generously. "There's no use in me hoping for it. I never can write a decent composition. But I hope you win, Nan!"

"Thanks," replied Bert's sister.

On the way home Nan told her brother how worried she had been when he was sent to the principal's office.

"I was worried myself, at first," Bert admitted. "But I had to laugh when he asked me to spin the top."

"I wish Mr. Tarton would send for me and ask me to turn somersaults in class!" laughed Freddie, when he heard his older brother and sister talking about what had happened. "I can do them fine—look!"

And on the grass at the edge of the sidewalk he flopped down and turned three somersaults one after the other.

"Good!" cried Bert.

"I can do that, too!" declared Flossie. "Want to see me?"

"No! No!" objected Nan. "You mustn't!

Not here on the street! You're a girl and
Freddie is a boy—that's different!"

"Well, I can turn somersaults as good as
he can!" declared Flossie.

But by this time they were nearly home,
and as Flossie was eager to see what Dinah
had for lunch she ran on ahead, forgetting
about the somersaults.

Around the lunch table that noon Bert
told about the spinning tops, and Nan spoke
of Miss Skell's offer of a prize for the best
composition on the summer vacation happenings.

"Mother, do you think anything will happen when we get to Cloverbank?" asked the
little girl eagerly.

"Many things may happen," was the answer. "I hope they will all be happy happenings, though; for you can just as well write
about them as about sad ones, I should
think."

"Oh, yes!" agreed Nan. "I want them to
be happy and funny."

The end of the school term was coming.
By Thursday the last examinations would
be over and then would come the closing
session.

It was all settled about the Bobbsey twins going to Cloverbank. Mr. Bobbsey had written to Mr. Watson, thanking him, his wife, and also "Baby May," for the kind invitation to come to spend the summer on the big country place.

"We will drive to Hitchville in the automobile," Mr. Bobbsey said, in talking over the plans. "Cloverbank is the name of Mr. Watson's farm, and it is just outside Hitchville."

"Will Dinah and Sam come with us?" asked Flossie, for she loved the dear old colored couple who had so long looked after the children.

"No, Sam and Dinah are going to have a vacation, too," Mrs. Bobbsey answered.

"Are we going to take Snoop and Snap?" asked Freddie, as he looked at the dog and the cat who were playing together out in the yard. The two were great friends.

"I fancy there will be many animals on Mr. Watson's farm, so there will be no need to take Snap and Snoop," Mrs. Bobbsey replied. "We will send our dog and cat away to be boarded for the summer as we have done before."

"Well, I'm going to take my fishing pole, anyhow," declared Bert.

"And I'm going to take my toy fire engine," declared Freddie. "The farmhouse might catch fire and I could put it out."

"Don't take too many toys," warned his mother. "Your engine is all right, and Flossie may take one of her dolls. But we haven't room for all your things."

It was not easy for the two smaller twins to leave their many playthings behind, and Flossie could hardly decide which of her many dolls she wanted with her. But at last the choices were made, Bert and Nan took what they wanted (Nan's choice was a book or two) and finally everything was packed ready to leave.

The last day of school came. Good-bye messages were exchanged and pupils and teachers separated to meet again in the fall, which now seemed a long way off.

"Don't forget about the prize composition!" called Miss Skell to her pupils.

"We'll remember!" promised Nan.

The Bobbsey twins could hardly wait for the hours to pass until they should be in the car and on the road to Hitchville. But at last the house was closed. Snap and Snoop had been sent away, not without many farewells on the part of Flossie and Freddie. Sam and Dinah had departed to visit relatives. Then away from Lakeport rolled the Bobbsey family.

"I hope a lot of things happen before we get back," remarked Nan to her mother. "I want them to put in my composition."

It was a pleasant day for the start of the trip. Mr. Bobbsey expected to reach Hitchville early in the evening.

Most of the morning had passed and they had covered nearly a hundred miles of the journey when came a question which was always asked, sooner or later, on all the trips the Bobbseys took.

"When do we eat?" demanded Freddie, about eleven o'clock.

"Why, you aren't hungry now, are you?" inquired his mother.

"Sure I am," he said. "I can eat a lot. And I wish I had a drink of milk."

"We didn't bring any milk along," said Mrs. Bobbsey. "I was afraid it would sour, the weather is so warm."

"I fancy we can get some milk to drink

with our lunch at that farmhouse," said Mr. Bobbsey, pointing to one a short distance ahead. "I see cows in the field back of it, and they must sell milk. We'll stop and inquire."

A basket of Dinah's best lunch had been put up to eat on the trip, and milk would make a welcome addition to it, Mrs. Bobbsey thought. Her husband was right in his guess about the farmhouse. When the auto stopped there the lady said they would be glad to sell as much milk as the children could drink.

"Bring your lunch in and eat it under the trees in the yard," she invited. "It's cool and shady there. I'll bring the milk up from the cellar."

"It will be nice to get out of the car for a change," said Mrs. Bobbsey, and soon there was a jolly little picnic party under the trees in front of the old-fashioned farmhouse.

The children would have been pleased to stay there most of the afternoon, to look about the place, but when lunch was over and each of the twins had had two glasses of milk, Mr. Bobbsey suggested that they had better travel on, as he did not want to arrive in Hitchville after dark.

Back into the car they climbed, and with many thanks to the good-natured farm lady, once more they were on their way. Flossie and Freddie were quieter now, as they always were after lunch, and even Bert and Nan did not talk as much as they had during the first part of the trip.

But soon the quiet of the journey was broken by Mrs. Bobbsey, who gave a little jump. Their mother was sitting in the rear with Flossie and Freddie. She exclaimed:

"There's something in this car!"

"Why, of course there is!" laughed her husband. "The whole Bobbsey family is in it!"

"No, I mean something else—something extra! Some kind of an animal!" insisted his wife. "I can feel it moving around my feet! Listen! What is it? Stop the car, Dick! There is some animal in it!"

CHAPTER VI

THE LONELY CABIN

MRS. BOBBSEY's voice showed that she was in earnest, so her husband lost no time in guiding the car to the side of the road, to be out of the way of passing autoists, and then he brought it to a quick stop with a grinding and squeaking of the brakes.

"Now what is it?" he asked, turning back to look at his wife.

"I said there was some strange animal— maybe more than one of them—in our car!"

"How could there be?" asked Mr. Bobbsey with a laugh. "That is, unless you call the twins animals, and they are—in a way."

"No, I don't mean them," answered his wife. "Oh!" she gave a little scream. "They're crawling around my feet. And listen to them!"

Now that it was quiet, Mr. Bobbsey, too,

63

could hear a faint whimpering sound. By this time Flossie and Freddie, who had dozed off into a sleepy little nap after lunch, awakened. They sat up, rubbed their eyes, and Flossie cried:

"What we stopping for? Are we at Cloverbank? I don't see any clover or any bank, either!"

"We stopped because your mother thought she felt and heard some kind of an animal in the car," explained Mr. Bobbsey, who did not know quite what it was all about, for he could see nothing as he looked over into the rear of the machine. But that he could see nothing was not to be wondered at, for the space was piled with luggage, robes, and things the children had brought with them, so there was scarcely room for Mrs. Bobbsey and the two small twins.

"I didn't *think* I felt or heard something!" said the children's mother in firm tones. "I *felt* something and *heard* something, and I feel it now! What is it?"

Then Freddie spoke up and said:

"I guess maybe it's the kittens!"

"Yes," agreed Flossie, with a little smile.

"It must be the kittens you feel, Mother. And I can hear them mewing now. Can't you hear the kittens mewing, Freddie?"

"Sure I can!" was the reply.

"Kittens? Kittens? What kittens?" asked Mrs. Bobbsey.

"It's the five little kittens Flossie and I put in a box and brought along with us," explained Freddie. "I guess they got out and it's them crawling over your feet, Mother."

"Five kitties can mew a whole lot," added Flossie.

"Five kittens! What in the world do the children mean?" cried Mrs. Bobbsey. She reached down into the midst of the baggage and other things and brought up a pasteboard box containing one lonely little kitten.

"I guess the other four are crawling around down there," said Freddie calmly. "There were five of them; weren't there, Flossie?"

"Yes, five," answered the little girl.

"I can feel them!" sighed Mrs. Bobbsey. "Oh, my goodness!" She reached down again, and one at a time, brought up four more kittens from the bottom of the car. She put them in the box with the other.

"Oh, aren't they cute!" cried Nan.

"One's almost as black as Snoop!" said Bert.

"Where in the world did you children get these kittens?" asked their mother.

"Back at the farmhouse," replied Freddie. "We thought we better have some animals to take out to Cloverbank in case Mr. Watson hasn't any, so Flossie and I put these five kittens in the box and put them in our car."

"There were six," added Flossie; "but we left one with the mother cat so she wouldn't be lonesome."

"Do you mean you youngsters packed these cats up back at the farmhouse where we got the milk?" asked Mr. Bobbsey.

"Yes, Daddy," assented Freddie. "We did."

"But don't you know that was a wrong thing to do?" reproved his mother. "These kittens weren't yours to take. They belong to some one at the farm where they were so kind to us."

"Yes," answered Flossie calmly. "They belong to the red-haired boy there. I asked him if the kittens were his and he said they were. Then Freddie asked him if we could have them and he said we could. Didn't he, Freddie?"

"That's what he did," was the answer. "So we took them."

"Well, I should say you did!" and now Mrs. Bobbsey could not help laughing. "But why didn't you ask me if you could do this?"

"We—now—we didn't want to bother you, because you always have so much to think about when we go on vacations," explained Freddie.

"So we just took the kittens," added his sister.

"Um! Yes! Well, we'll have to take them right back," said Mr. Bobbsey. "Perhaps that red-haired boy didn't know what he was talking about, children, when he said you could have the kittens. They may not have been his to give away, and the farmer or his wife may want them to catch mice in the barn. Yes, we must take the kittens back!"

"Oh, couldn't we please keep just one?" begged Flossie.

"The little black one that looks like Snoop!" pleaded Freddie.

But both Mr. and Mrs. Bobbsey were firm

—the kittens must go back where they came from.

"Though it will delay you to turn about and go to the farm, won't it?" Mrs. Bobbsey asked her husband.

"A little," he replied. "But it cannot be helped. However, the roads are good and we can make a little faster time the remainder of the day. I wish we didn't have to, but I feel that it is the best thing to do—take the kittens back."

Flossie and Freddie felt a bit sad over this, and even Bert and Nan would have liked one of the pets. But they thought their father and mother knew best.

"Very likely Mr. Watson will **have** plenty of animals at Cloverbank," said **Mrs.** Bobbsey, to console the sorrowing small twins.

"And, anyhow, there's the baby," said Nan.

"That's so," agreed Flossie. "I guess maybe it's better that we don't keep the kittens, Freddie. They might mew in the night and wake up Baby May—I mean Baby Jenny."

"I guess so," assented her twin brother.

So the auto was turned about and the return trip made in good time. The farm lady was rather surprised to see the travelers again.

"Did you come back for more milk?" she asked.

"No, thank you," said Mr. Bobbsey, with a laugh. "We came to return some of your property that my small twins thoughtlessly took."

"My property!" exclaimed the lady. And how she laughed when Mrs. Bobbsey handed her the pasteboard box of kittens! "Oh, my land sakes! You could have kept these, and welcome!" she said. "We have all the cats we want."

"I'm afraid we could hardly look after them," explained Mrs. Bobbsey. "Thank you, just the same. Dear me, when I felt them wiggling at my feet, I couldn't imagine what they were!"

"I can well believe that," said the farm lady. "Well, I'll give old Mary back her family," and she restored to the mother cat the squirming, hungry kittens and Flossie and Freddie viewed with delight how eager the five were to snuggle down in the warm basket with the one little pussy that had not been taken away.

"Now you haven't hidden any more animals in the car, have you?" asked Mr. Bobbsey, as he made ready to start again.

"No more," declared the small twins, and Mrs. Bobbsey looked to make sure no stray puppy had crawled in among the things.

Perhaps, because Mr. Bobbsey was in a hurry to make up the time and distance lost by returning to the farmhouse, he missed a side road altogether, or perhaps it was because he took a wrong turn at some crossroad in the journey, but certain it was that, late in the afternoon when he came to a signboard and read the names of the towns printed on it, he said:

"We must have come the wrong way."

"What do you mean?" asked his wife.

"We aren't on the road to Hitchville," was the answer. "To get there we have to pass through Midvale, and this sign doesn't say anything about that place. I must have taken a wrong turn."

"It is getting late, too," remarked his wife.

"No harm is done, though," said Mr. Bobbsey. "I will ask the first person I meet which is the best road to Midvale. Once we are there, I can easily find the way to Hitchville."

"Shall we get there to-night?" asked Nan.

"Why, of course we shall," declared her father.

As a matter of fact, he concluded later that he was not as sure of this as he wished he could be. But there was only one thing to do, and that was to go on until they met another autoist or some one of whom they could inquire.

For a mile or so the road was deserted. But presently, on making a turn, the Bobbseys saw coming toward them a farmer, driving a bony horse drawing a rickety old wagon.

"Hello there!" called Mr. Bobbsey, halting his car.

"Whoa—up!" the man directed his horse, and the animal seemed glad enough to stop. "Afternoon, stranger," greeted the farmer. "Are you looking for some one?"

"I'm looking for the road to Midvale, so I can get to Hitchville," explained Mr. Bobbsey. "Or perhaps you know of a short cut to Hitchville."

The farmer shook his head.

"No, there isn't any short cut," he said. "You'll have to go to Midvale, as that's the only place where there's a bridge over the river within ten miles. But you're 'way off the road to Midvale, even—'way off!''

"That's what I was afraid of," commented Mr. Bobbsey. "What shall I do?"

The farmer considered matters for a moment and then replied:

"Well, if I was you I'd keep right on this road until you get to the next highway. Turn to the right there and keep on for about five miles and you'll come to the road that takes you to Midvale. After that you'll be all right."

"Yes, after that I'll be all right," agreed Mr. Bobbsey. "But how about this road and the next—are they pretty good?"

"The roads are good enough," replied the farmer, as he looked at the Bobbsey twins. "But they're quite lonesome. However, you can go faster in that machine than I can in mine, and it won't take you long. Good luck to you! You've got quite a load of boys and girls there," he commented.

"Yes, quite a load, thank you," answered Mr. Bobbsey.

"We had five kittens, only we had to take them back," piped up Flossie.

"Did you? Well, I've got a batch of 'em

out at my place I'll let you have," chuckled the farmer. "Just keep right along as I told you an' you'll come out all right. G'lang!" he called to his horse, and with a nod he drove by, while Mr. Bobbsey, with a word of thanks, let in the clutch and away they rode once more.

"It's too bad!" murmured Mrs. Bobbsey.

"Are we lost?" asked Freddie, half hoping they were.

"Of course not!" laughed his father. "We'll soon be in Midvale, and it isn't far from there to Hitchville. We'll be all right. But I don't call this a very good road," he went on, as he had to slow up over a rough and rutty place.

The farmer's idea of good roads did not seem to be the same as Mr. Bobbsey's, and the farther they went the worse the way became, until in one place it was necessary to drop into second speed to get through a stretch of deep sand.

It was now getting late in the afternoon, and they had not yet come to the road which, the farmer said, led to Midvale. Then, to make matters worse, all at once there was a sharp hiss of escaping air.

"Puncture!" cried Bert.

"So it is!" sighed his father. "Well, luckily we have a spare on, and it won't take long to change."

But it took longer than he thought, for the road was sandy, and the jack, for lifting up the car so the tire could be changed, sank deeply into the soft earth. By the time some boards and flat stones had been found to put under the jack, it was getting dusk.

"You'll hardly have the tire changed before it's dark," said Mrs. Bobbsey with a look around the lonely road.

"I'm afraid not," agreed her husband. "But we can drive after dark, you know."

"I don't like it much—on strange roads," she said. "I wish there were some place where we could stay, but there doesn't seem to be."

Nan, who had gotten out to walk around with Flossie and Freddie while Bert helped his father, now came back with the small twins in time to hear what her mother said.

"There's a house just around the turn in the road where we might stay," said Nan.

"A house?" inquired her mother.

"Yes. A log cabin. Come, I'll show it to you!"

"Shall I go and look?" asked Mrs. Bobbsey of her husband.

"Perhaps you had better," he agreed. "This tire is harder to change than I thought. I'm afraid it's going to take a long time. But I can't imagine there is any place around here where we could put up for the night. Still, it will do no harm to look. Hand me that wrench again, Bert, please."

Mrs. Bobbsey and three of the children walked around the turn in the road.

"There it is," said Nan.

She pointed to a lonely cabin set a little way back from the highway. It seemed very quiet—deserted, in fact—and as she looked at it Mrs. Bobbsey felt a chill in her heart.

"I don't like the looks of that!" she said. "I'm afraid we could never stay there. No one lives in it, and it's such a lonely place!"

Flossie and Freddie drew closer to their mother while the shadows of night settled down about the lonely cabin.

CHAPTER VII

THE NIGHT CAMP

MR. BOBBSEY knew it was going to be hard work to get the spare tire on the car and start off again in the darkness to find Midvale. He walked down the road a short distance to where his wife and the children stood. Bert went with him.

"The best thing for us to do," said Mr. Bobbsey, when he reached his wife's side, "will be to stay here all night. It's too risky going on now—the road is too bad, and I can't see very well to change the tire. We'll stay here!"

"Stay here?" repeated Mrs. Bobbsey.

"Bert and I can sleep in the auto," went on her husband. "We have often done it."

"But there isn't room for all of us!"

"You and Flossie and Freddie can sleep in that cabin," went on Mr. Bobbsey. "It will be a good shelter and it isn't going to rain, so it won't matter if the roof leaks, and it looks as if it might, the place is so old. We have some auto robes with us, and the night is going to be very warm."

"Do you really mean I should stay in that lonely cabin with Flossie and Freddie and Nan?" asked Mrs. Bobbsey.

"Why not?" asked her husband. "We have camped out in worse places than that, and so have the children."

"I like it!" declared Flossie. "Maybe there's a kitten in the cabin."

"I like it, too," said Freddie, always quick to side with his twin sister. "We'll pretend we're Indians!"

"Let's take a look at the place and see if it's as bad as it appears," suggested Mr. Bobbsey. "Of course if it is too terrible, we'll try to get the spare tire on and move along."

"Oh, I don't want to give you too much trouble," Mrs. Bobbsey was quick to say. "But at first glance that place looked sort of —well, lonesome. Perhaps it will be all right. Let's go and look," she concluded.

Once they were inside the cabin, it was not

as bad as it appeared from the outside. True, it was lonesome. The cabin, made of logs, stood by itself in a weed-covered field and there were no other houses within sight.

There was nothing in the place save some broken boxes and some bunks, like low, broad shelves, built against the sides of the smaller of two rooms. There were only two rooms in the place, and no upstairs. In one of the rooms there was a fireplace.

"Would you be afraid to sleep here?" Mr. Bobbsey inquired of his wife. "We could cut some branches from the evergreen trees outside and spread them on the bunks. They would be a sort of spring and mattress together. Then with the auto robes you would have a pretty good bed."

"Yes, I guess it would be all right," assented his wife. "We'll stay. It's the only thing we can do," she added, with a look at the gathering darkness outside. Indeed, night had now come and only that Mr. Bobbsey had brought a big electric flashlight in with him from the car they could have seen little in the lonely cabin.

"Well, then, come on, boys!" called their

father to Bert and Freddie. "We'll gather evergreen boughs and make the beds."

"I'll help," offered Nan.

"So will I!" chimed in Flossie.

"No, you stay with Mother, dear," suggested Mrs. Bobbsey. "You can help me make a fire. I'll just build a little blaze on the hearth," she told her husband. "It will give us light to see and make it more cheerful."

"There's another flashlight in the car," he said.

"Better save that," advised his wife. "A little blaze of pieces of the old boxes will do very nicely."

When the blaze was crackling up the chimney, built of field stones, the inside of the lonely cabin was very cheerful. Mr. Bobbsey and Nan and the boys brought in armfuls of the sweet hemlock branches and piled them on the wooden bunks which contained not even a shred of a blanket.

"When are we going to eat?" asked Freddie, when this work had been done.

"Yes, I'm hungry," added Flossie.

"We shall have supper—such as it is—right away," answered Mrs. Bobbsey. "Luckily Dinah put us up a big basket of food."

When a sort of bed had been arranged for Bert and his father in the auto, where they would have to lie curled up "like puppies," as Freddie said, and when the robes had been brought in to spread under Mrs. Bobbsey and the children, who would sleep in the cabin bunks, then the basket of food was opened.

Not much had been taken out for the noon lunch, and plenty of sandwiches and other good things remained for the evening meal.

They sat on broken boxes about the blaze on the hearth and ate, becoming quite cheerful and gay in spite of having to camp out so unexpectedly.

"Do you think Mr. Watson will worry because we don't get there to-night?" asked Nan of her mother, when the meal was over.

"No; for I didn't say exactly when we would get to Cloverbank," answered Mr. Bobbsey. "I told him when we would start and said we hoped to reach Cloverbank the same evening. But I did not say we would certainly do so."

"It's a good thing you didn't," remarked Mrs. Bobbsey. "We never expected to have to do this. But I rather like it," she went on, with a laugh.

"It's lots of fun," said Freddie.

Flossie said nothing, but from her manner it was easy to see that the little girl was tired and sleepy. Freddie, too, was "fighting the sandman," as his father called it, and so, after making sure that his wife and the three twins would be as comfortable as possible, Mr. Bobbsey and Bert went out to the auto to pass the night.

Mrs. Bobbsey had one bunk to herself, Nan took Flossie in with her, and Freddie had the third bunk, thus using all there were in the cabin. At first the little boy wanted to stay with his father and Bert in the car, but his mother had said:

"But what shall we do without a man to look after us in the cabin?"

"Oh, I'll stay with you!" Freddie had quickly replied. "You needn't be afraid of anything when I'm here. I'll get a big stick and keep it by my bunk, and if I hear a noise in the night I'll get up and hit it!"

"Do you mean you'll hit the noise?" asked Bert, with a laugh.

"I'll hit the thing that makes the noise!" declared Freddie.

So the Bobbsey twins had made a night camp, and, once the first notion of loneliness was gone, it was not bad at all, Mrs. Bobbsey declared.

The small children were soon asleep, and Nan was not long in following them to Dreamland. Mrs. Bobbsey, however, could not so easily drop off to slumber, and Mr. Bobbsey did not find the auto as comfortable as he had hoped.

Bert, however, was a healthy boy. He had often camped out, and could curl up almost anywhere and go to sleep. So he, too, was soon slumbering peacefully.

Just what it was awakened Freddie the little fellow afterward said he did not know. But several hours after having gone to bed on the hemlock boughs something caused him to open his eyes with a start. At first he could not remember where he was, it was so different from awakening in his comfortable bed at home. But when he saw a faint glow of the fire on the cabin hearth, then he remembered.

"Oh, we're camping out on the way to

Cloverbank," whispered Freddie to himself. In the other bunks he could hear the gentle breathing of his mother and sisters. Then came again the noise that had startled the little boy into wakefulness.

It was a noise as if some one were moving something in the darkness—moving something there in the cabin. It was not Freddie's mother nor Nan nor Flossie, for they were lying in their bunks. The little boy could see them by the faint glow of the embers.

Then came the rattle of wood, as if one of the broken boxes was being dragged over the floor.

"Oh, I guess it's Daddy come in to put more wood on the fire," thought Freddie, with a sigh of relief. "Is that you, Daddy?" he asked in a loud whisper.

There was no answer, but the noise ceased. And Freddie knew that if it had been his father preparing to put more wood on the fire, he would not have stopped because Freddie spoke.

"No, it can't be Daddy!" thought the little fellow.

Then he heard the noise again, louder than before. A piece of box was being dragged across the floor, and Freddie could hear the scraping of feet—feet like those of an animal.

Freddie was a small boy, but he knew enough to be sure it could be no large or dangerous animal like a bear or a wolf. No such animals were left in the woods so near towns and villages. But it was *something*, and what it was Freddie felt he must find out.

"I'll throw my club on the fire," he told himself. "That will blaze up and I can see what it is."

True to his promise, the little boy had placed a piece of dry wood—part of a box— near his bunk when he went to bed. This stick was to "hit a noise," as Bert laughingly said. Freddie now reached down, felt on the floor until he found this wood, and then he slipped off the bunk and started toward the glowing fireplace.

But he had not taken more than three steps when he stumbled over something and fell down with a crash which awakened his mother who cried:

"What is it? Who is there? What has happened?"

CHAPTER VIII

THE STORM

SILENCE followed the noise of Freddie's fall and his mother's questions. But it was silence for only a moment. The commotion awakened Flossie, who caught hold of Nan, with whom she was sleeping, and called out:

"What's the matter?"

"I don't know, dear," Nan answered quietly, for she did not want Flossie to be frightened. Indeed, Nan, as yet, knew nothing about which to be alarmed. True, there had been a noise, but that often happened at night, even at home.

Mr. Bobbsey, out in the car with Bert, also heard the sounds in the cabin, his wife's voice having awakened him.

"I'm coming!" he cried, jumping out of the car. None of the campers had taken off their clothes.

"So am I!" added Bert, as he followed his father.

By this time Freddie had "picked himself up," as he said afterward, and discovered that he had stumbled over a broken box in the middle of the cabin floor. The little fellow was not hurt.

Also by this time Mrs. Bobbsey had reached for and turned on the flashlight her husband had left with her, so that she could see what had caused the commotion.

What she saw was Freddie standing with his "club" in his hand, ready to cast it on the embers, so there would be blaze enough to see what had caused the noise. But the gleam of the electric torch made Freddie's brand unnecessary now.

"What is it, Freddie?" asked his mother. "Did you fall out of bed?"

"No, Mother, I didn't fall out of bed," answered the little lad. "I got out to make the fire brighter so I could see."

"See what?" asked his father, who, by this time, had come into the log cabin, followed by Bert. "What did you want to see, little fireman? Tell me!"

"Little fireman" was a good name for

Freddie in this case, as he was about to start the fire to blazing again.

"I wanted to see the noise," stated Flossie's brother.

"Ho! Ho!" laughed Bert. "You can't *see* a noise."

"Well, I wanted to see what made it," went on Freddie. "I heard a noise and it woke me up."

"Did the noise wake you, too, Mother?" asked Nan.

"Well, some noise did, but I think it was Freddie falling out of bed that I heard," answered Mrs. Bobbsey.

"I didn't fall out of bed!" insisted Freddie. "I got out all right, and then, in the dark, I fell over one of these old boxes. It was a noise like one of these broken boxes being dragged over the floor that I heard. There it goes again!" he cried, pointing to a dark corner of the cabin. "Listen!"

Mr. and Mrs. Bobbsey each held a flashlight now, but the beams were turned away from the corner toward which Freddie pointed so that it was quite dark over there. Truly enough, a noise had come from there.

Quickly Mr. Bobbsey pointed his light in

that direction and an instant later there was a scurrying of feet and a rattle of wood.

"Look! It's a dog!" cried Freddie.

"Or maybe a skunk!" shouted Bert. "Better be careful!"

"No, that wasn't a skunk," said his father. "It was a dog, and he seemed to be dragging that broken box, which would have made the noise which Freddie heard."

The dog had quickly run out, and when Mr. Bobbsey went over to the corner, where it seemed to have been hiding during the excitement, the reason for it all was explained.

Caught in one corner of the broken box was a bone with some meat on it. Perhaps the dog himself had put the bone there during the day and had come back in the night to get it. But the bone had become wedged fast and in pulling on it the dog moved the box over the floor.

"And that's what made the noise that awakened Freddie," said Mr. Bobbsey, when he had finished looking in the corner. "The dog came back here to get the midnight lunch he had hidden, for it is midnight and past," Mr. Bobbsey went on, looking at his watch.

"Well, I'm glad it was only a dog," said Mrs. Bobbsey. "He may come back and disturb us again, for the door is so broken that it cannot be tightly shut," she added.

"But I can toss the dog's bone outside so he will not need to come in after it," said Mr. Bobbsey. "That will keep him outside. And since there is a dog around here I believe we aren't as far from a house where people live as I thought at first. There may be a settlement just over the hill. We'll find out in the morning. Now we can all go back to sleep."

This they did, and nothing more disturbed them until the sun was shining in the morning, when it was t me to arise.

Mr. Bobbsey's guess, about people living just over the hill, was correct. He and Bert, walking to the top of the hill and looking about, saw several houses not more than half a mile from the lonely cabin. At one of these houses Mr. Bobbsey arranged for his family to have breakfast.

"Have you got a dog?" asked Freddie of the farmer, whose wife had agreed to set a morning meal for the travelers.

"Yes, we have a dog," was the answer.

"At least, he stays here some of the time, but mostly he roams around nights. There he is now—been out all night, as usual," and with a laugh the man pointed to a small black and white dog that came into the yard, wagging its tail in a friendly fashion.

"That's the dog that made a noise in the night when I fell over the box!" declared Freddie, and Bert said it was the same animal that had come into the cabin after the bone.

"It would be just like Major," chuckled the farmer. "So you stayed all night in the old cabin, did you?"

"Yes," answered Mrs. Bobbsey, as she sipped the hot, comforting coffee the farmer's wife set before her. "Did anybody ever live there?"

"A queer, solitary sort of fellow—a farm hand," answered the farmer. "But that was some time ago. It's too bad you folks didn't come on just a bit farther and you could have spent the night here."

"We couldn't get any farther with a flat tire," said Mr. Bobbsey. "Besides, from the lonely look of that cabin, it didn't seem as if there was another house within ten miles."

"Yes, it is lonesome back there by the cabin," agreed the farmer. "But that fellow liked it lonesome, he said. Do you want me to hitch up and haul your car here?" he asked.

"Oh, no, thank you," replied Mr. Bobbsey. "Now that it is daylight and I can see what I'm doing, it will be easy enough to change the tire. Then we can go on to Midvale and thence to Hitchville. This road will take us to Midvale, will it not?"

"It will if you keep on going long enough," the farmer said. "But you missed the best and shortest way. However, there's no help for it now. I hope you don't have any more bad luck."

"Thanks," said Mr. Bobbsey.

The twins, as usual, finished their meal before their father and mother were ready to leave the table, and, being excused, they ran out to see and make friends with Major, the dog, who was ready enough to play with them. There were other farm animals, also, to be admired. A little lamb, its mother dead, was being brought up on a baby's feeding bottle by one of the farm boys. The little "cosset," as a lamb of this kind is called, was so "dear and sweet" that the children begged their father to buy it for them.

"I guess you'll find something just as good at Cloverbank," he said, with a laugh. "Anyhow, we haven't any room for it in the auto."

"And I doubt if my Ned would sell it at any price," said the farmer. "He sets quite a store by that cosset."

So the Bobbsey twins had to leave without it, and probably it was just as well, since the auto was quite filled as it was.

The sunshine gave plenty of light for Mr. Bobbsey to see to change the tire, and in a little while the travelers were riding along again after the night of adventure.

Midvale proved to be a pleasant little village. Here a stop was made to get some gasoline and oil, and then once more the Bobbseys were on their way.

The road to Hitchville was a main one, well traveled and with signs up in many places, so there was no more danger of Mr. Bobbsey taking the wrong turn. The children began anticipating their arrival, and were talking about what they would do when they reached

Cloverbank, which they hoped to do by early afternoon.

But when Nan saw her mother and father now and then turning to look up at the sky, the Bobbsey girl thought something might be amiss, so she asked about it.

"I think we are going to have a storm," her father replied. "I don't like the looks of those clouds."

On and on they journeyed, going a bit faster now that the storm seemed approaching more rapidly. Fortunately the road was a good one. As they went down a little hill toward a white bridge, they saw a boy on it jumping up and down, seemingly much excited. He was shouting something and pointing down toward the water.

"Somebody may have fallen in!" cried Mrs. Bobbsey. "Stop the car, Dick, and find out!"

"I will!" was the answer, and the auto came to a halt on the bridge, close to the jumping, excited, shouting boy.

"What's the matter?" called Mr. Bobbsey, hurrying from his seat behind the wheel. "Is somebody in the water?"

"Yes! Yes! There she is! She can't

swim, either!" cried the boy. "Oh, get her out!"

"Is it your sister?" asked Mrs. Bobbsey, as she put aside some valises and bundles to enable her to get out.

The boy did not answer, but kept shouting and jumping around, meanwhile pointing to the water. Mr. Bobbsey looked over the railing of the bridge, but when he saw no child in the stream, which at this point was wide and deep, he turned to the boy and said:

"What's the matter with you? There's no one in there!"

"Yes, there is!" cried the lad. "It's my cat! She followed me down the road and when an automobile ran close to her on the bridge she tried to climb up on the rail and she fell in! Oh, please get her out before she drowns!"

Mr. Bobbsey looked again, and, sure enough, saw a cat trying to swim to shore. But cats aren't like dogs. Their fur gets so wet when they are in the water that it is hard for them to get out again. Bert was going to ask why the boy himself didn't get his own cat out, but when the Bobbsey lad saw how small the other lad was, he held back the question. Instead Bert cried:

"I'll get her for you!" He ran down off the road toward the edge of the river.

"Be careful!" warned his mother. "You may fall in or get stuck in the mud!"

But Bert was taking no chances. He picked up a piece of tree branch, and, leaning over the edge of the stream, while he held to a bush, he reached the branch out and pulled the poor cat to shore. With pitiful mewings and looking very wet and miserable, the pussy crawled out.

"Oh, thanks!" cried the boy.

"You're welcome," answered Bert, with a laugh.

The boy ran down and picked up the cat, all dripping wet as it was, in his arms. Evidently he loved animals, and if he had not been so excited he, himself, might have rescued his pet as Bert had done.

"I thought a child had fallen in," said Mrs. Bobbsey.

"So did I," agreed her husband. "But if we don't hurry along we may all be as wet as that kitten. It's going to rain hard soon And with this wind it will be a driving rain so the top on the car won't be much protection. It's too much work to get up the side curtains. We'd better run for shelter."

Leaving the boy with his wet cat calling out renewed thanks to Bert, the Bobbsey family started off once more. Now the sky was torn with jagged flashes of lightning, followed by low mutterings of thunder which seemed to come nearer and nearer.

"I guess this is Hitchville," said Mr. Bobbsey, as they turned off a country road into a town. Very soon several signs told them that this guess was correct.

By this time the wind was blowing hard, the lightning was more vivid, and the thunder louder.

"Hadn't we better run into some garage here?" asked Mrs. Bobbsey of her husband, as they passed along the main street of Hitch-ville.

"Wait until I find out how far it is to Cloverbank farm," he suggested. "We may be able to get there before the storm breaks if it isn't too far."

He stopped to make inquiries of a traffic officer where the two main streets of Hitch-

ville crossed, and the officer said Mr. Watson's place was about two miles out, on the
main road.

"We can make it!" decided Mr. Bobbsey.
"It won't rain for ten minutes yet and we'll
be there before then."

But they had no sooner gotten beyond the
town than the first drops began splashing
down, to the accompaniment of loud thunder
and such glaring lightning as to make Flossie
hide her head in the auto robes.

"It's going to pour in another minute!"
cried Mrs. Bobbsey. "I wish we had stayed
in Hitchville!"

"Yes, it would have been better," agreed
her husband. They were on the main road
now, but there was no shelter in sight until,
as they made a turn, they saw just ahead of
them a farmhouse and a large barn up a lane
and near the road. The wide doors of the
barn were open, and as there came a sudden
burst of rain and a great crash of thunder,
Mrs. Bobbsey suggested:

"Drive into that barn, Dick. Then we'll
be sheltered. Don't try to go on to Cloverbank."

"All right," he replied, speaking loudly to

be heard above the noise of the storm. "I guess that's the best thing to do!"

He swung the auto off the road, into the lane, and up the inclined drive right into the open barn, much to the surprise of two men who were inside, having evidently gone there for shelter.

A moment later it seemed as if the sky were torn open to let down the rain which dashed around the barn in a fury, whipped by the high wind, while the lightning flashed and the thunder rumbled.

CHAPTER IX

"Thank goodness, we're in a dry place!" exclaimed Mrs. Bobbsey with a sigh of relief, as the car came to a stop within the shelter of the big barn.

"It doesn't rain in here, does it?" asked Freddie.

"Of course it doesn't," declared Nan, with a laugh.

"It rains on the roof of the barn. I can hear it!" said Flossie.

The children, who had been a bit cramped by the long auto ride and somewhat wet by the dashing rain, now prepared to get out of the car. They wanted to watch the storm from the safe shelter of the farm building.

The two men, who had, it seemed, also taken shelter there from the downpour, had been looking curiously at the Bobbsey family.　Seeing this, Mr. Bobbsey smiled and said:

"I hope the owner of this barn won't mind my driving in like this."

"Oh, no, the owner won't mind a bit," answered one of the men, with a laugh. "You're perfectly welcome."

"Do you happen to know the owner?" asked Mrs. Bobbsey.

"Well, yes, I might say I do," went on the man who had first spoken. "I know him quite well."

"I should say you did!" chuckled the other man.

"We are on our way to a place called Cloverbank," said Mr. Bobbsey. "We are going to stay there for the summer. I think it is near here."

"Oh, yes, it's right near here," went on the man who had said he knew the owner of the barn. "In fact, it couldn't be any closer; could it, Zeek?" and he nodded to his companion.

"It's about as close as you can get to it," declared the other.

Just then Mrs. Bobbsey gave a little cry of delight and exclaimed:

"Oh, now I know you! I was wondering where I had seen you before! You are Mr. Watson himself!" and she walked forward and held out her hand to the man who had first spoken.

"Is this Baby May—I mean Baby Jenny's father?" asked Nan.

"That's who I am!" was the laughing reply.

"And is this Cloverbank?" demanded Freddie.

"That's what it is, little man!" said Mr. Watson. "You drove right in on us. This is one of my barns, and I'm glad Zeek and I had the doors open so you could roll right in. Welcome to Cloverbank! I wish you could have arrived in better weather," he continued, as a vivid flash of lightning came and a heavy peal of thunder seemed to shake the ground. "But I think the storm will soon be over."

"I hope so!" exclaimed Mrs. Bobbsey. "But just fancy us, turning right in here! It's remarkable!"

"Zeek and I had to run for it ourselves," explained Mr. Watson. "I had left the doors open to dry out some early hay I had hauled in, and Zeek—his name is Zeek Trimmer and he works for me," he explained, as the hired man nodded, "Zeek and I were working around outside, when, almost before we knew it, the rain came down in bucketfuls. So we had to run to the barn."

"And then you folks came along," added Zeek, who seemed a very pleasant sort of person. The Bobbsey twins thought they were going to like him very much.

"I'm very glad to see you again, Mr. Watson," said Mr. Bobbsey as he shook hands with the farmer. "I didn't know you at first. I guess I must have had some rain in my eyes. How is Mrs. Watson and Baby May—I mean Baby Jenny? We all have a habit of calling the little girl by the name we gave her," he explained.

"That's all right," laughed the farmer. "She's fine, and so is my wife. They'll be mighty pleased to see you. We'll go to the house as soon as this rain lets up. You can leave your car right here for a while. Afterward we can run it to the garage. But you're a little late, aren't you?"

"Yes, we were delayed on the road," explained Mr. Bobbsey, and he told of the happenings on the trip, how they had had to go back to return the five kittens, and then how they had had to stay all night at the lonely cabin.

"Well, we're glad to see you, anyhow," returned the farmer. "Zeek and I will bring your things in," he went on, as he saw Mrs. Bobbsey beginning to take articles out of the car.

"I guess I better carry my doll," explained Flossie. "You might drop her, Mr. May— I mean Mr. Watson," she quickly corrected herself.

"All right, little lady!" chuckled Baby Jenny's father. "I'm used to carrying my own little girl, and I don't drop her; but maybe your doll is so heavy she might slip out of my arms. Though I could wrap her in a bundle of hay and carry her like that," he added, as he caught up a wisp of hay from the barn floor and pretended it was a doll.

"Oh, yes, you could carry her that way," admitted Flossie. "But I guess I'd better take her myself—though thank you just the same," she added after a moment of thought. Then she took her doll, which her mother handed out of the car.

"And I'll take my fire engine," said Freddie. "That might get smashed." He hauled his toy out from amid the valises and packages, and as he set it on the floor he went on: "It squirts real water, Mr. Watson, and if your barn gets on fire I can help put it out for you."

"That's right kind of you," said the farmer, trying not to laugh, for Freddie was very much in earnest. "I hope my barn won't get on fire, though."

Just then came a tremendous crash of thunder, following closely after a bright glare of lightning.

Mr. Watson went over near Zeek Trimmer, who stood just inside the door, to look out and see if the lightning had done any damage to his farm buildings or the house, which the children could see through the rain, a short distance away.

"I guess that was the last crack, and the worst," said the farmer. "It will stop in a little while, and then we can go to the house. Mrs. Watson has been expecting you, but she never thought you would come in a downpour like this."

While the older folks stood in the middle of

the barn floor, talking, the children wandered
about the big barn. They always liked to
come to the country, especially to a farm, for
there were so many strange bits of machinery
to see and so many things to do about a
barn.

"Mr. Watson! Mr. Watson!" called Freddie, who had put his toy fire engine down in
what he thought a safe place.

"Yes, little man, what is it?" asked the
farmer.

"Could we please slide down on your
hay—I mean Flossie and I?" Freddie asked.
"We like to slide on hay, and we haven't
done it for a long time."

"Slide all you like," Mr. Watson kindly
gave permission. "That is, if your mother
says so," he added, with a look at Mrs. Bobbsey.

"I guess they won't get hurt," she remarked.

"Well, they can't harm the hay!" chuckled
Zeek.

So the two smaller twins, with shouts of
delight, climbed up in the haymow where
there were great piles of the dried, sweet-
smelling grass which the horses, cows, and

sheep would eat when winter came, and when there was no longer green fodder in the fields.

Bert and Nan thought themselves a little too old for this kind of fun—at least, when there were older folks around. Though undoubtedly if just the four twins had been in the barn, the two larger ones would have enjoyed doing what Flossie and Freddie were doing.

These two scrambled up to the highest point of one of the hay piles and then slid down, the hay being almost as slippery as a hill covered with snow.

Bert and Nan wandered about the barn, looking at the different things. Bert wished there were some horses he might view, but the farm animals were kept in another building, this large one being used for the storage of hay and other crops.

Presently Nan, who was peering about along the edge of the hay mow, gave an exclamation of surprise.

"What's the matter?" asked Bert.

"Look!" whispered Nan, pointing down through a small opening in the floor. "There's a hen on her nest. Maybe she's laying an egg!"

"Maybe," agreed Bert. "If she is we mustn't disturb her."

But the hen was already disturbed, for she looked up and saw the children and then, with a loud cackle, she fluttered off the nest and ran across the barn floor.

"Oh, I didn't mean to scare her!" murmured Nan.

"You didn't do any harm," said Mr. Watson, with a laugh. "That's Old Speck, as we call her. She always steals away to make a nest for herself, lays a lot of eggs in it and then hatches out a brood of chickens. I've been trying for a week to find her nest. Show me where it is. Are there any eggs in it?"

"Oh, a lot of them!" cried Nan.

"About a dozen," reported Bert.

"Then she's getting ready to hatch out a family of little chickens," Mr. Watson said. "I'll be on the watch for them, now that I know where she has hidden her nest. It's queer you found it so soon, Nan, when I've been looking for it a week and couldn't find it."

"I guess maybe the wind blew away some hay that was over the top, and that's why I saw her," explained the little girl, and this seemed to be about the way of it.

"Well, I'll put a board over the hole from the top, so she won't be disturbed again," Mr. Watson said. "Get aboard, Zeek. Old Speck must crawl in under the barn to get on her nest, so the board won't shut her out."

The rain was lessening now, and the lightning was not so sharp nor the thunder so loud. All signs pointed to a clearing off of the storm. Meanwhile, Flossie and Freddie were having fun in the hay until, all of a sudden, Flossie gave a scream of excitement and cried:

"There! Now look, Freddie Bobbsey, what you did! You've killed her!"

"Gracious!" cried Mrs. Bobbsey. "I hope Freddie didn't slide down on the hen," for Nan had told about finding Old Speck.

"He slid right on my doll, that's what he did!" cried Flossie. "He slid on her, and he sat on her, and he's killed her! Oh, dear!"

She was about ready to burst into tears, but Nan, running to Freddie, who sat on the barn floor in some hay which had slid with him off the big pile, picked up Flossie's doll and called out:

"She isn't hurt a bit! See! She's all right, Flossie!"

"Will her eyes open and shut?" asked the little girl.

"Surely they open and shut," reported Nan, tilting the doll backward and then forward, which caused the blue eyes to close and then to open.

"Well, then, I guess she's all right," Flossie agreed, choking back her tears. "But you oughtn't to have sat on her, Freddie Bobbsey!"

"How could I help it?" Freddie asked. "I didn't mean to do it! I just slid with a lot of hay. I didn't know you had put your doll down there."

"Well, I had," Flossie said. "But I'm glad you didn't mean to hurt her. I guess we've had enough of hay-sliding, anyhow."

"I guess so, too," agreed Freddie. "Anyhow, the sun is shining now and we can go to the house. I want to see the clover bank."

"And I want to see the baby," added Flossie.

The storm, indeed, had ended and the weather was clearing. With Mr. Watson, Zeek, and Mr. Bobbsey carrying the baggage, and the children taking their toys and play-things, the party moved on toward the big farmhouse. On the porch stood Mrs. Watson.

"Well, of all things!" she cried, as she caught sight of the Bobbsey family. "How did you folks get here?"

"We came in the storm and drove right into your barn, not knowing whose it was," explained Mrs. Bobbsey.

"How glad I am to see you!" went on Mrs. Watson, as the children and the others trooped up the front steps. "We have been expecting you—in fact, we looked for you yesterday."

"And we would have been here then, only for the many things that happened," explained Mr. Bobbsey. "It is very kind of you and your husband to ask this whole family out here for the summer."

"We're glad to have you," said Mrs. Watson.

"Where's the baby?" asked Nan.

"You mean Jenny?" asked the mother. "Oh, she's in the house. She's grown so you will hardly know her," she went on proudly.

"Can she talk?" Freddie wanted to know

"A little, yes, my dear," was the answer.

"Can she walk?" was Flossie's question.

"She's just beginning to, yes. And that reminds me. She may get up and walk into some mischief now. I hardly dare leave her alone, she is so active, Mrs. Bobbsey. You'd hardly believe the——"

But Mrs. Watson did not finish what she was saying. She was interrupted by a loud noise from within the house. Instantly she turned and ran inside, crying:

"Oh, Baby! Baby! What have you done now?"

CHAPTER X

FREDDIE'S CRASH

SOMEWHAT alarmed by the crash, Mrs. Bobbsey and the others followed Mrs. Watson into the house. Mr. Watson, who, with Zeek and Mr. Bobbsey, had just arrived from the barn with some of the baggage, rushed in, exclaiming:

"My land, sounds like that youngster has had another fall!"

"Does she fall much?" asked Mr. Bobbsey.

"About three times a day, on the average," explained the father. "But she's very lucky —she hardly ever gets hurt. You see, she has just found out she can walk, and she takes too many chances."

"I hope nothing has happened," said Mr. Bobbsey.

A moment later they heard Mrs. Watson's laugh from within the house and all felt sure that matters were all right.

"Oh, my dear, what a fright you gave me!" Mrs. Watson could be heard saying.

"What happened?" asked her husband, as his wife appeared carrying the little one.

"Oh, she just pulled over a chair and upset the basket of empty spools we keep for her to play with," explained Mrs. Watson. "You ought to see how cute she looked, wondering what it was all about."

"Mustn't pull over chairs!" playfully warned Mr. Watson, as he held out his finger, which the little one grasped with a smile of delight. "You might break the furniture!"

"Break the furniture! As if that mattered!" cried his wife. "She might have hurt herself!"

"My, how she has grown!" exclaimed Mrs. Bobbsey, taking the baby from its mother.

"She's getting to be a big girl," added Mr. Bobbsey. "She doesn't look like the little stranger we found on our doorstep."

"Cloverbank is a good place for children to grow up in," remarked Mr. Watson. "Yours will be so big when they go back to Lakeport the neighbors won't know them."

"Well, I only hope they don't grow out of their clothes," said their mother, with a laugh. "I didn't bring many suits with me."

By this time the Bobbsey twins were gathered about Baby Jenny, or, as the smaller children often called her "Baby May."

"Isn't she cute!" murmured Nan.

"May I hold her?" begged Flossie.

"Yes, a little while, if you will sit down in a chair so you won't drop her," Mrs. Watson promised. Baby Jenny seemed glad to see the visitors and smiled and "jabbered" at them, as Bert said afterward, though the baby's mother said:

"Just listen to her talk, would you? Isn't she bright?"

"Indeed, yes!" agreed Mrs. Bobbsey.

"Could you understand what the baby said?" Bert asked Nan a little later.

"Not a word," was the answer. "But I guess all babies talk like that. Only their mothers can understand them."

Meanwhile Flossie, much to her delight, was allowed to hold the little one in her lap.

"It'll be your turn pretty soon, Freddie," said Flossie to her brother, for as the two smaller twins always shared everything they had or did, naturally Flossie thought her small brother would want a part in holding Baby Jenny.

"I guess I rather let her play with my fire engine," Freddie said, squirming around on one foot. "I don't zazackly know how to hold babies."

"Well, I wouldn't want you to drop mine!" laughed the mother. "But make yourselves at home, folks," she went on. "My, you must be tired with your long trip and sleeping in a cabin and then getting here in the rain. But it's clearing off beautifully now," she added.

So through the rooms of the big, pleasant farmhouse they went, and soon they were all made to feel at home by the kindness of Mr. and Mrs. Watson, not to mention the smiles and cooings of the baby.

The weather had cleared, following the heavy thunderstorm, and gave promise of many fair days to come.

"Won't we have fun here?" said Bert to Nan, as the two put on their play suits ready to go out and explore the place.

"It's just lovely!" Nan said. "I'm so

glad we came! I've got a lot of things to write about for my composition already."

"What composition?" Bert inquired.

"The one we are going to write to try to win the prize Miss Skell offered," explained Nan. "Aren't you going to write a composition about what happens this summer, Bert?"

"Oh, maybe," he replied, not much interested, it appeared. "But I have to see something happen first."

"Why, a lot has happened already!" exclaimed Nan. "There were the five kittens, and sleeping in the lonely cabin, and then the thunderstorm, and us not knowing it was the Cloverbank barn we drove into, and Mrs. Watson thinking the baby was hurt— all those things have happened and we haven't really begun yet."

"Oh, if you call *those* happenings—yes," agreed Bert. "But they aren't any good to put in a composition to win a prize."

"Of course they are!" insisted Nan. "The teacher said it was better to write about the common, everyday happenings, if we did it well, than to try to write about something big we didn't know anything about."

"Um! Maybe," admitted Bert. "But

there's plenty of time. We have all summer ahead of us. I'll write my composition the last week when I see what has happened."

"I'm going to write down the different things that happen every day, and then I'll pick out the most interesting and write about them," decided Nan. "I do hope I win that prize!"

"I hope you do, too," said Bert kindly. "I guess I won't try for it, and then it will be easier for you."

"Oh, no, you must try, too," declared Nan, and Bert said he would think it over.

Meanwhile, the other Bobbsey twins, who had also put on their everyday clothes, had come down to wander about the place to discover what there was with which they could play and have a good time.

"But I want to see the clover bank," insisted Freddie. "Where is it?"

"There it is, little man," said Zeek Trimmer, who was passing on his way back to the barn. The hired man pointed to a side hill not far away. It was green with growing clover which was washed clean by the recent rain.

"I don't see any bank," Freddie stated.

"There's a bank at home in Lakeport where Daddy puts his money. But I don't see any place where they put clover."

"Ho! Ho!" laughed Bert. "I guess he thought the clover bank was a building like the money bank at home."

"Well, isn't it?" Freddie inquired.

"No, dear," explained Nan. "That's just a bank, or hill, of dirt, and the clover leaves and blossoms grow on it. I suppose it's such a big bank, or side-hill field, of clover, that Mr. Watson named his farm Clover-bank. Isn't that it?" she asked the hired man.

"That's it," was Zeek's reply. "We've got the best field of side-hill clover on any farm for miles around. And we've got the best peach orchards, too," he added proudly.

"Oh, do you grow peaches?" cried Bert.

"I should say we do. They're almost ripe, too, and we'll begin picking in a few days."

"Does Mrs. Watson can the peaches?" Nan asked, for she had sometimes helped her mother at preserving time by washing the glass cans.

"There's more peaches at Cloverbank than

Mrs. Watson could ever can," said Zeek. "Come and I'll show you."

With shouts of delight the Bobbsey twins followed the hired man, Flossie and Freddie already feeling so friendly with him that they had hold of his hands.

"Where are you going?" called Mrs. Bobbsey from the porch.

"I'm just taking them to one of the peach orchards," answered Zeek.

"Is there more than one orchard?" asked Bert, in surprise.

"Oh, yes," the hired man replied. "Mr. Watson has several large ones. Part of his business is raising peaches for the market. We'll begin picking and shipping soon."

Zeek took the children to one of the orchards where there were many rows of small trees, each one laden with peaches, many of which were beginning to show the yellow, pink, and red cheeks which told they were nearly ripe.

"And over the clover hill are more orchards, just like this," the hired man said. "Now let's see if we can find a few ripe ones."

He picked a few, but would not let the

children eat any until they were back at the house, when Mrs. Bobbsey gave permission for each of the twins to have one.

"If you eat any more you won't be hungry when meal time comes," said Mrs. Watson.

"I guess I'd be hungry if I ate five peaches," declared Bert. "I have a big appetite to-day."

"I'm glad of it," said Mrs. Watson, with a laugh. "Then you'll appreciate the roast chicken."

"Oh—chicken—goodie!" cried Flossie and Freddie.

At the table a little later, not only Bert, but the other three Bobbsey twins proved that they had good appetites. It was a delightful meal.

The afternoon was spent in going about the farm, viewing the different buildings, fields, and peach orchards, and when night came four tired but happy children were ready for bed, where Baby Jenny had long since gone.

The next few days were happy ones. There seemed something new to do from the time the children were up in the morning until the sun went down at night. The twins were out of doors all day long, for after the big thunderstorm the weather was delightful.

"When are you going to pick peaches?" asked Bert of Mr. Watson at the dinner table one day.

"I think we'll begin to-morrow, if it doesn't rain," was the answer. "I have advertised for help, and if the day is fair the pickers will be here by sunrise, I expect."

This is what happened, and when the children awoke, some time after sunrise, however, they looked upon a busy scene. A number of men and women and some large boys and girls had arrived to help gather the peach crop.

"Oh, let's go down and see them!" cried **Nan.**

As their mother and father were as interested as the twins, soon the whole Bobbsey family were in one of the orchards.

In among the rows of trees were tall stepladders, and standing on these the pickers plucked the ripe fruit, putting the peaches into cloth bags that hung about their shoulders. When the bags were filled, the pickers climbed down and emptied the fruit into big boxes that stood about.

While some were doing this, other workers sorted out the best peaches into baskets which were put on a motor car and hauled to the big barn into which Mr. Bobbsey had driven the day of the storm.

"In the barn," Mr. Bobbsey explained to the children, "the peaches are sorted again, wooden tops are fastened on the baskets, and they are then hauled to the big peach market in a distant city where they are sold."

"Oh, could we go to the peach market?" asked Bert.

"Perhaps," his father said.

"Why don't they just shake the trees and let the peaches fall on the ground and then pick them up?" asked Freddie.

"That would never do," said his father. "The peaches would become bruised by falling on the ground, and once a peach, apple, or other fruit is bruised it rots very quickly. Great care must be had in picking the best fruit if it is to be sold for a good price in the market. See how careful the pickers are."

But in spite of all the care used, there were soft and bruised peaches. Some fell off the tree before they could be picked. These soft peaches were put in a separate bin.

They could be sold to a near-by canning factory to be made into marmalade, the soft parts being cut out.

It was a busy and entertaining sight in the peach orchard, and as Nan looked on she said to Bert:

"I'm going to put this about peach-picking in my composition."

"Well, I'm going to put a peach into myself," said Bert, with a laugh.

"I wish we could help pick," said Nan, after a while, and Mr. Watson, passing through the orchard, heard this and said:

"Of course you can help. Here, Zeek, put them at one of the low trees where they can reach without a ladder."

And, to their delight, the Bobbsey twins, even Freddie and Flossie, were soon helping gather the peach crop. They picked the fruit carefully, put it in bags which were given them, and carried the full bags to the big boxes.

Then something happened. Freddie, not content to stand up on a box and reach the fruit just over his head, saw, not far away, a tall stepladder. Saying nothing to his brother or sisters about it, the little fellow slipped away by himself, and when Nan looked for him she saw him up on top of the ladder reaching up into the higher limbs of a peach-laden tree.

"Freddie! Freddie! Come down off that!" ordered Nan.

And then Freddie came down, but not in just the way Nan intended. For he reached too far to pick a red peach, overbalanced himself, and, a moment later, over went the ladder with a crash, little boy and all.

"Oh! Oh!" he cried.

"Oh! Oh!" gasped Nan.

"Look out!" shouted Bert.

CHAPTER XI

BERT HAS AN UPSET

WITH a thud Freddie crashed down. But instead of hitting the hard ground, he fell into a box of soft peaches, and it was like falling on a load of hay—almost. In fact, some of the peaches were so soft that Freddie was smeared with the pulp and his face and clothes were stained with the juice.

"Oh, Freddie Bobbsey!" cried his mother, who had come up in time to see her little boy fall.

"I—now—I couldn't help it, Mother! Really I couldn't!" protested Freddie, as he tried to climb out of the box of soft peaches.

"I know you couldn't help it, my dear," his mother said, as she and Bert helped him to climb over the edge of the box. "But you should never lean too far to one side when you are up on a ladder. Oh, Freddie, you are a sad sight!" she sighed as she looked at his soiled garments. "And Mr. Watson's peaches! Oh, dear!"

"Freddie looks like a peach short-cake," remarked Nan.

"More like a long-cake," declared Bert. "He's got peach pulp all over him."

"Well, they're my old clothes, anyhow," said Freddie, as if that helped some, which it probably did.

"Did you get any peach in your mouth?" asked Flossie.

Freddie moved his tongue around over his teeth to make sure.

"No, I guess I didn't," he answered. "But I'll go up to the house and wash, Mother, and put on other clothes, and then I can help pick more peaches, can't I?"

"I guess you'd better stay on the ground or on a box which isn't so high as the ladder, and then you won't fall next time," suggested Mr. Watson, with a laugh.

"Did he do any damage?" asked Mr. Bobbsey, who came up from another part of the orchard in time to see Nan leading her small brother back to the house to help him change his clothes.

"No damage at all. He fell in the soft peaches that are going to the factory where they will be made into peach butter," answered the farmer. "For canned peaches, either in halves or slices, the canning factory, of course, uses only good, sound fruit. But the soft ones, when they aren't actually rotten, can be made up into peach butter, and very good it is, too. No, Freddie didn't do any harm."

The work of gathering the peaches was in full swing now, for it was the time to gather the best of the crop and sell while the prices were high.

"Where do you sell your fruit?" asked Mr. Bobbsey of the farmer when Freddie had returned to the orchard.

"Over in Hitchville," was the answer. "There's a peach market there, where the wholesale buyers come and buy them by the truck load. I'll have about two loads ready to go in to-morrow."

"Could we go with you and see how they sell peaches?" asked Bert, who hoped, when he grew up, to become a business man like his father.

"Yes, you children can ride on the truck

if you like," the farmer said. "But you'd be more comfortable going in your own car. The trucks are big and heavy and aren't easy riding."

"I'll take the whole family over in my car," Mr. Bobbsey said.

"And it will give me a chance to do a little shopping at the Hitchville stores," Mrs. Bobbsey said. "I need some things for the children."

So the trip was planned for the following day, by which time many peaches would be picked by the orchard workers. After a while the Bobbsey twins became tired of "helping," as they called it, and they had eaten all the peaches that were good for them, so they turned to look for something new to amuse them.

"Why don't you go up in the barn and watch them sorting the peaches?" suggested their mother. "That will be fun."

"Oh, let's!" exclaimed Flossie. "And we can roll on the hay."

But just then Bert saw a small cart drawn by an old and slow-going horse being driven into the orchard by Zeek. Bert at once had an idea.

"What's that cart for, Mr. Watson?" the boy asked.

"We use that to cart the soft peaches in, as it doesn't do much harm if they get shaken up and bruised a bit more," the farmer answered. "We have to be more careful with the sound fruit, and I send that up to the barn on my small auto truck. But we don't much care what happens to the soft peaches."

"Do you think—now—maybe—if I was careful—I could drive the cart back to the barn?" asked Bert eagerly. "I'd love to drive the horse, and I know how, for I did it once when we were at Meadow Brook. Could I, please, Mr. Watson?"

"There won't be any danger driving this horse," chuckled Zeek, as he brought the animal to a stop near the box of soft peaches into which Freddie had toppled. "He'll stand without hitching any minute of the day or night."

"Do you think it would be all right for Bert to take in a load?" asked Mr. Watson of his hired man.

"Oh, sure!" was the answer.

"I'll be very careful!" promised the small boy.

"Well, wait until I load the truck and you can take charge," suggested Zeek, one of whose duties was to transport the soft peaches to the barn and later to the canning factory after they had been sorted.

Meanwhile Nan had taken Freddie and Flossie to the big barn where a number of men were engaged in the work of carefully sorting the best peaches into several grades.

"Well, all right," said Mr. Watson, as he moved on to visit another of his orchards. "I'll leave this to you and Zeek, my boy."

Delighted at doing what seemed to be real work, as it was, in a way, Bert helped Zeek put into baskets the best of the soft peaches from the box of discarded ones. Some were so soft that it would not be wise to take them to the barn. These very soft ones and some that had been crushed or broken by falls were put in another box and later fed to the pigs and chickens.

When the small cart was loaded Zeek told Bert how to drive to reach the barn and also told the boy what to do when he got there.

'Aren't you going to ride with me?" asked Bert, for he thought the hired man would at least be with him on the cart.

"No, I'm not going," was the reply. "Land sakes, I guess you can manage a load of soft peaches all right, 'specially when Tramper is hitched to the cart."

"Yes, I guess I can," Bert assented. "Is the horse named Tramper?" he inquired.

"That's his name," replied Zeek, with a laugh. "I named him that myself," he added.

"Won't Nan and the others be surprised when they see me driving up all alone?" exclaimed Bert, with a happy laugh as he climbed up to the seat of the cart and looked at the pile of soft peaches behind him.

"Well, don't give 'em too much of a surprise," advised Zeek.

"Do you mean Tramper might run away?" the boy asked.

"Oh, no danger of that!" chuckled the hired man. "But don't upset the cart before you get to the barn. After you get there it doesn't matter much what happens."

"Oh, I won't upset!" promised Bert. "I know how to drive."

For a time all went well. There was a level road leading into and out of the orchard, and along this Bert guided the steady old horse. On either side were men and women up on ladders picking the peaches, and Bert felt that they were all looking at him as he went along.

"Go on there, Tramper!" he called to the horse. But the patient old animal did not pay much attention to anything. He never went a bit faster for all Bert's talk.

The lad guided the horse and cart safely out on the main road, and along that to the lane which led to the barn where the sorting was going on.

As Bert hoped, Nan and the smaller twins were in the doorway and saw him coming.

"Oh, look at Bert!" cried Flossie.

"He's driving a real horse!" added Freddie.

"So he is!" exclaimed Nan.

Bert "began to put on airs," then, as his father said later. But just as he was urging the horse up the little slope that led into the barn, Bert saw a turtle crawling across the lane in front of him. The wheels of the cart would almost surely pass over the turtle's shell, crushing it.

"Look out there, Mr. Mud Turtle!" cried Bert. But the turtle, like all of its kind, was a slow mover. It did not get out of the way.

Bert pulled sharply on the left rein to turn the horse and swerve the cart. But he pulled too hard. The horse turned too suddenly, and the cart began to tilt to one side.

"Oh, Bert!" screamed Nan, who was watching.

Then, before he could swing the animal the other way, over went the cart, Bert, peaches, and all in a grand upset.

CHAPTER XII

FLOSSIE'S BEAR

MR. BOBBSEY, who had gone to the barn before Bert left the orchard driving Tramper, now ran out of the building, somewhat alarmed and fearing his son might be hurt. But Bert had been thrown a little distance from the cart and had landed safely on a clump of soft grass at the side of the lane, so he wasn't hurt at all.

As for Tramper, he didn't seem to mind it in the least. He just stood still when he felt something wrong happening, and he let the cart go over. In fact, he could not have stopped it had he wished.

"Bert, why in the world did you turn so sharply?" asked his father, as he ran over to pick up the boy. But Bert did this for himself. "You shouldn't have made such a sudden turn," went on Mr. Bobbsey.

"I know it—now," Bert ruefully answered as he looked at the peaches scattered over the ground. "But I turned so I wouldn't run over a mud turtle."

"Well, of course that was a kind thing to do," went on his father. "But a slower turn might have saved the turtle and also saved the cart from upsetting. However, it can't be helped now."

"Bert tipped over! Oh, Bert, you tipped right over, didn't you?" gasped Flossie.

"I sure did," answered her brother, trying to smile.

"And you spilled the peaches, didn't you?" went on Freddie. "Didn't you spill the peaches, Bert?"

"I guess anybody can see that," Bert said.

"What will Mr. Watson say?" asked Flossie.

"I don't know," answered Bert. "But you two run into the barn now and I'll pick 'em up."

"We'll help," kindly offered Flossie.

"Course we will!" added her twin brother.

"It won't take long with all of us helping," put in Nan.

Mr. Bobbsey, with the help of some of the men who were sorting peaches in the barn, turned the cart over on its wheels again, and then began the work of tossing back into it the spilled peaches.

"No great harm done," said the man in charge of the sorting. "These are bruised peaches anyhow, and a few more knocks won't make 'em any worse. It's a good thing you were driving Tramper instead of a livelier horse, my boy," he continued, "or he might have run away when he felt the cart going over."

"Yes, I'm glad Tramper stood still," Bert rejoined. The horse had begun to eat grass after the accident, as much as to say that it wasn't his fault and he didn't care how long they took to load the cart again.

But at last the spilled fruit was gathered up and once more Bert mounted the seat and took the reins. For Mr. Watson, arriving from a distant orchard and hearing about the accident, had said that Bert·was to try again.

"You might as well learn now as any time not to turn a wagon too suddenly," he said kindly to the boy. "Get up and try again.

I'll watch you and tell you if you turn too short."

So Bert had a lesson in driving, and he was glad Mr. Watson had not been angry because of the upset. But the farmer knew that young people must have a chance to learn, and so he was patient.

"Whoa!" called Bert, as he drove Tramper into the barn with the load of soft fruit and stopped the cart where Mr. Watson told him to. Then the fruit was put into wooden bins and the sorting went on.

"Do you want to bring in another load?" asked the farmer.

"Do you think it safe to trust him?" inquired Mr. Bobbsey. "I don't want him to make a lot of work for you."

"He can't hurt the soft peaches much, anyhow," the farmer went on, "and there's nothing like letting a boy know how to handle a horse. He'll be safer with Tramper than any other animal. Go on, Bert, drive back to the orchard and get more peaches."

"Could we ride with him?" begged Flossie.

"Oh, let's!" called Freddie.

"Well, we'll all go," said Mr. Bobbsey. "I used to know how to drive a horse, and if

Bert gets into any trouble I can help him out. But don't upset this load, son," he warned with a laugh, as he put the small twins into the cart, while he helped Nan up and then got in himself. They sat on boards placed across the high sides of the cart.

"I'll be very careful," promised Bert.

The turtle, which had been the innocent cause of the other accident, crawled off in the high grass around the barn. Bert started Tramper back on the trip to the orchard, and this time he made the return with a load of peaches in safety, driving proudly into the barn, almost as well as one of the men could have done.

The barn and the orchard were now busy places, for Mr. Watson wanted to get as much fruit to market as he could while the weather was good. He expected to make two or more pickings, as more and more peaches were ripened by the sun. And the earlier he could haul his fruit to market the more money he would get.

"It's the early fruit that sells best," he said.

The sorting went on in the big barn, basket after basket of choice yellow and red peaches being packed, covered, and set in a cool place, ready to be taken the next day on the big truck to Hitchville. There there was quite a large peach market, where buyers came from the big cities miles away to bargain for the fruit.

"And we're going there to-morrow!" sang Flossie that night, after a day of fun, part of which was spent in the peach orchard.

"Are we going to take Baby May—I mean Baby Jenny?" asked Nan of Mrs. Watson.

"No," was the answer. "She will be better off at home. I have told your father that Jenny and I are sorry to decline his nice invitation to go along. But when she gets as big as you I expect she will help her father gather the peaches," she added, as she cuddled the baby in her arms.

The next day was a fine one, the sun shining down from a sky of blue with white clouds floating here and there like sailing ships.

"Well, everything looks well for a big peach crop," said Mr. Watson, as the truck was started off on the road to Hitchville.

As the truck would have to travel more slowly than the faster pleasure car, Mr. Bobbsey would not leave Cloverbank for several minutes yet. At the end of this time the Bobbsey twins and their father and mother were on the highway, over which they had come a few days before in the driving rain storm.

"You take the children out to the peach market, and I'll do some shopping," Mrs. Bobbsey told her husband. "You can stop for me on the way home."

The peach market was in a big open lot near a railroad siding, on which stood many freight cars. Even before the children reached the place they could smell the sweet perfume of the peaches.

And such a busy place as the peach market was! At first Bert and the others could make little of it. There were so many motor and horse-drawn trucks, so many men shouting back and forth, so many freight cars with an engine puffing up every now and then to haul them away—there was so much confusion that the Bobbsey twins did not know what it was all about.

A man would jump up on a box or a barrel and shout something. Other men would shout something back at him. Then they would wave their hands, they would write down something on pieces of paper, and move away. Then the same thing would happen in another place.

"What are they doing?" Nan asked her father.

"Selling loads of peaches by auction to the highest bidder," was the answer. "There is Mr. Watson—watch him."

The children saw their farmer friend standing up on the seat of his big motor truck, which was piled high with baskets of peaches, some of which the children had picked. About Mr. Watson's truck were gathered a number of men, some of whom were lifting the edges of the covers over the baskets to look in at the kind of peaches grown at Clover-bank.

Then followed much talk and shouting, until at last Mr. Watson was heard to exclaim:

"Sold! Where do you want them?"

"Take them to that car!" directed a man, hurriedly writing something on a piece of paper and giving it to the farmer.

"Mr. Watson has just sold his load of peaches," explained Mr. Bobbsey. "Several buyers offered different prices for them, after seeing what fine fruit he had, and Mr. Watson sold to the man who would give him the most money. He will now put his peaches into a freight car and later they will be hauled by the engine to some distant city. There they will go to what is called a wholesale dealer. He has bought them here, through his agent or a commission man, as he is called. The wholesale man will sell them to stores and the stores will sell them to people who want a quart or a single basket. That is how the peach business is carried on."

"When I grow up," said Freddie, as he looked at all that was going on, "I guess I'll be a peach-man instead of a fireman!"

"Oh, so you've changed your mind, have you?" laughed his father. Ever since he was a small lad Freddie had said, many times, that he was going to be a fireman. No toy pleased him more than a little engine or a hook and ladder truck. But now he seemed to have a different idea. "Well, we'll see— when you grow up," laughed his father.

They had lost sight of Mr. Watson now, but guessed, as was the fact, that he had gone to unload his truck load of peaches into the box car. Soon they saw him again, his truck empty, and he waved his hand to them and called:

"Back now for another load!"

"Good luck to you!" wished Mr. Bobbsey.

After remaining a little while longer to view the busy scenes in the peach market the Bobbsey twins were taken back to Hitchville, where they met their mother, who had finished her shopping.

"Well, did you have a good time?" she asked.

"Fine!" answered Bert.

"And I was going to be a peach-man. But I guess I'll be a fireman like I always was," Freddie told her.

"Perhaps that will be best," his mother agreed, with a laugh.

Back to Cloverbank drove Mr. Bobbsey and his family, and there they found the picking and sorting of peaches still going on.

"Let's watch 'em sort peaches in the barn," suggested Bert.

The work was now going on faster, for Mr. Watson wanted to take advantage of the good weather and the high prices fruit was bringing. After a while Flossie and Freddie, in the spirit of investigation, wandered down to a lower floor of the big barn.

"What place is this, do you s'pose, Freddie?" asked the little girl, as she pointed to a small door in the side wall.

"I don't know," Freddie answered. "Maybe it's a sort of icebox, where Mr. Watson keeps peaches over night."

"Maybe," Flossie said. "I'm going to look in and see."

She tried to open the door, but it stuck, and she called to Freddie to help her. Together the children managed to open it, the workers in the barn paying little attention to the twins, for there was no work going on near this door. No sooner was the door opened, allowing Flossie to enter a little way, than she gave a scream and cried:

"Oh, there's a bear here! Look at the bear! Oh, Freddie!"

She darted back so quickly that she knocked Freddie down.

CHAPTER XIII

NAN'S TROLLEY RIDE

"What's that you said, Flossie? Where are you going?" asked Freddie, scrambling to his feet.

In her excitement over what she had seen, Flossie had screamed in such a shrill voice that her brother hardly understood her.

"What's the matter? What are you running for?" he called to her.

"I guess you'd run yourself, if you saw a bear!" panted Flossie. She could not run very fast, for the passage, like a wooden tunnel, was covered on the bottom with wisps of hay, and that made it slippery.

"A bear!" gasped Freddie. "Did you see a bear?"

By this time he and Flossie had gotten out of the passage and were back in the big barn, on the other side of the small door they had opened. There was no one else near them, none of the peach workers, nor was Bert nor Nan. The small twins had this part of the barn to themselves.

"Yes, it was a bear," declared Flossie, not so excited, now that she saw a door between herself and the beast. "It wasn't a very big bear," she added. "Just a little bear."

"I'm going to look!" declared Freddie, for, unlike his sister, he was not afraid of wild animals like bears, wolves, and lions. At least, Freddie said he wasn't.

"Oh, you mustn't go in there!" exclaimed Flossie, when she saw her brother about to open the small door. "The bear will get you! We'd better go tell Daddy or Mother."

"I don't believe there's a bear in there," asserted Freddie. "How could a bear get here, anyhow? Bears don't eat peaches."

"Well, maybe they eat hay, and there's lots of hay in this barn," Flossie said. "And I heard Mr. Watson say he was going to put more in soon. Maybe the bear wants hay."

"Bears don't eat hay," went on Freddie. "They eat people. But I'm not afraid of a bear—anyhow, not of a little bear. And I don't believe there's a bear here. They stay in the woods."

Flossie knew that, as a rule, bears did do this. But she was sure she had seen some queer beast. So she ran to Freddie as he was trying to open the door and cried:

"Don't go in! Don't go in! If it wasn't a bear it was some terrible wild animal! Let's run!"

But Freddie wanted to show off before his sister, to prove how brave he was.

"The bear won't hurt me!" he insisted. "You stay back there, Flossie, but I'll open the door and look at him. And if it's a big bear I'll go call Mr. Watson. He has a gun— I saw it in the house."

Flossie got ready to run farther back in the barn, and Freddie was tugging at the door, which had swung shut rather tightly, when he was spared the trouble of opening it. The door opened itself! Or perhaps something on the other side pushed it open, and the two children saw a strange beast staring at them. It was a creature with a black, bushy head, and at the sight of it Flossie cried:

"There! It is the bear! It is the bear! Now you'd better run, Freddie Bobbsey!"

"Yes, it's a bear all right!" gasped the boy. "And it's a big one, too! I'll go get Mr. Watson and his gun!"

The two children ran out of a side door of the barn. Some distance away from that part of the building where the peaches were being sorted they saw Zeek, the hired man, walking toward them.

"Oh, there's a bear in here!" screamed Flossie.

"A big bear!" added Freddie, as if that explained why he was also running. For he didn't want it known that he would retreat from a small bear.

"What's that you say?" asked the hired man. "A bear?"

"In the barn," added Flossie.

"He came out of the little door," went on Freddie.

"Oh, you mean in the fodder tunnel," said the hired man. "Well, there can't be a bear there."

"But we saw him!" insisted Flossie.

"And he had a black, bushy head," explained her brother.

Zeek, laughing and shaking his head,

entered the barn, followed by the two
children.

"Hadn't you better get a gun?" asked
Freddie.

"No, I guess your bear will come and eat
out of my hand," said Zeek.

"Oh, is he a trained bear?" Flossie wanted
to know. She was not frightened now, and
Freddie's courage, also, came back to him.
Zeek did not answer, but led the way to the
fodder tunnel door. The children followed
him.

Then, just before reaching the place, they
were startled by a loud:

Maa-a-a-a!

"There's your bear," chuckled Zeek. A
moment later a half-grown calf ran toward
him and Flossie and Freddie! But it was
not like any calf the children had ever seen.
Its head was large and black and bushy.

"What makes him look so queer?" asked
Freddie, as the calf, again uttering its maa-a-a
cry, began nosing Zeek's hand as if seeking a
taste of salt, of which all cattle are very
fond.

"Why, this calf has been roaming around

the pasture lot," explained the hired man, "and he's got a lot of burdock burrs and other stickers all over his head. No wonder he looked like a bear. My, but you are a sight, Sukie!" he said to the calf, to which, he explained later, he had given that odd name. "I'll have to get a curry comb and brush and clean you up," he went on, as he began pulling the burrs from the animal's shaggy head.

"Is that all it was—a calf?" asked Flossie.

"That's all," said Zeek.

"It looked like a bear," Freddie remarked.

Both children, but especially Freddie, felt a little disappointed, now their fright was over, to find that their "bear" was only a calf.

"I haven't the least doubt of that," chuckled Zeek, in answer to Freddie's remark. "He's got a head almost as big as a buffalo's."

This was true. Sukie had rambled into one briar and burr patch after another. Then he had found his way down near a lower part of the barn connected with the fodder tunnel. The calf had gotten into this tunnel, which was used as a passage way from one part of the building to another. And, pushing along, the calf, with his head looking like a "bear" as Flossie thought, had confronted the little girl.

When she and Freddie ran back into the main barn, the calf followed them, and, hoping to get something to eat, possibly, had pushed the door open.

"It will be a week before you look like yourself again," said Zeek to the calf. "But I suppose you didn't know any better. Well, I'll turn you out where you belong," and he led the calf to a side door, and a little later the children saw the hired man using a curry comb on the creature.

Never was there such a jolly place to have fun as Cloverbank. Not only was there the big farmhouse with its attic containing many wonderful things, but there were barns, an ice-house, a smokehouse, and many other buildings where all sorts of games could be played. The attic alone would keep the children busy two or three rainy days at least, Mrs. Watson said.

But, as yet, the Bobbsey twins had done no more than peer into the delightful attic. While the sun shone they wanted to be out of doors, and for the first week of their visit to the farm the weather was fine. It was just what was needed to allow the peach crop to be gathered.

In the days that followed the experience of Flossie and Freddie with the "bear," the children often visited the orchards, where they helped pick the red and yellow fruit. At other times they would help sort it in the barn, and once they rode with Zeek to the canning factory with a load of soft peaches which must quickly be made up into marmalade lest they spoil.

One day, when a lull came in the hard-and-fast work of picking and sorting the peaches, Nan, passing through the kitchen, saw Mrs. Watson getting ready to make some biscuits.

"Oh, may I do that?" begged Nan. "I know how! Mother showed me! Didn't you?" she asked Mrs. Bobbsey who just then came into the kitchen.

"Yes, Nan bakes very good biscuits," was the answer.

"I'd be glad to let her bake mine," returned Mrs. Watson. "The baby is so fretful to-day she doesn't want me to leave her. So go ahead, Nan; and I wish you luck."

"You'd better wish her something else," put in Bert, with a laugh.

"What do you mean?" asked Jenny's mother.

"I mean you'd better wish that Flossie doesn't sit down in the batch of biscuits," Bert went on. "Flossie did that to Nan's biscuits the time we were keeping house last winter," and he explained what had taken place, as has been related in the book before this one.

"That will never happen again!" said Nan. "I'll watch where I put the pan of biscuits, and I'll watch Flossie. She won't sit in any more of them!"

"Well, in that case, I'll let you do the baking," promised Mrs. Watson, and soon Nan was in her element. She loved to cook and she really knew how to make very good biscuits. And as Flossie and Freddie were playing at sailing boats down in the brook, the little twin girl and boy did not appear on the scene to cause trouble.

Nan's biscuits came out of the oven a lovely brown, and when Mr. Watson asked for a third helping of them at the table when supper was served, Nan felt just a little bit proud, as well she might.

"The best biscuits I ever ate, except those

my wife makes!" said the farmer, with a laugh.

Mr. Bobbsey had to return to Lakeport to see about some business matters, but he planned to return to the farm as soon as he could. He would have to make trips back and forth that way all during the summer, he told his family.

It was the day after Mr. Bobbsey went away that Nan strolled out to the large barn in time to see a big wagon loaded with hay drive into the yard. She saw several men, a horse, a long rope, and what looked like a big iron letter U turned upside down near the hay wagon.

"What's it all about?" asked Nan.

"That's the hay fork and unloading trolley," explained Zeek, who was busily hurrying to and fro. "You see we have such a lot of hay that some of it has to be stored in the top story of the barn. It would take too long to carry it up, one pitchfork full at a time, so we have this hay fork. It's like the letter U turned up, as you see, and on each of the legs, as you might call them, are prongs which fold up when they aren't in use. A man jabs the two ends of the U down into the hay.

Then he pulls on a rope and that makes the prongs stick out and they hold a big bundle of hay.

"Then the horse starts walking along the ground and he pulls the hay fork full up to the top of the barn over a pulley wheel. The horse does most of the work, you see, and we can put in a lot of hay in a short time."

Nan watched as the fork took up what seemed to be a quarter of the load on the wagon, and then, as the horse pulled, up the mass of dried grass rose in the air.

Then it rolled along by means of a grooved trolley wheel on a tight rope until it reached the open door of the second story of the big barn. Into the door went the mass of hay, and a man there pulled on another rope, loosening the prongs in the legs of the U and the hay fell out. Then the empty fork coasted back down the inclined stretched rope until it was at the wagon again.

Nan found this very interesting to watch, and in order to see better she climbed up to the top story of the barn and found herself in the hay mow which was being filled.

"Hello! who's there?" asked Zeek, as he heard some one behind him. Zeek had gone up to empty the hay fork after each full trip.

"I came up to watch," said Nan.

"All right—stand over there and you'll be safe," said the hired man.

As one wagon was emptied of its load in this quick fashion, another drove into the yard, and the fork began taking the hay off that. Then some one called Zeek away and Nan was left alone in the mow. As she stood there the horse on the ground below started off, raising a fork full of hay and pulling it toward the open mow door.

"Oh, dear!" exclaimed Nan. "Here's a lot of hay coming and no one to open the fork. I wish I could do it. I think I could. I watched Zeek. All he does is to pull the short rope. I'll do it!"

And so, when the fork full of hay swung into the barn, Nan made a jump for the dangling short rope and pulled on it. But the hay fork did not open. Something was caught, or jammed. Nan fairly lifted herself off the ground in her eagerness to pull, and hung dangling by the rope fast to the fork full of hay.

Just then Zeek, who had gone out of the

barn, looked up and saw the fork full of hay in the open door.

"What did you haul that up for?" he asked the man, who was driving the horse. "I'm not there to open the fork!"

"Oh," said the man, "I didn't know that. I thought you were there. I'll let the hay come back again!"

He spoke to the horse. The animal began backing, and the big bundle of hay began to roll down the inclined trolley rope.

As it came out of the barn Zeek and the others were startled to see Nan Bobbsey clinging to the rope. Before she could let go she was being given a dangerous hay trolley ride out of the barn, high in the air over the yard.

"Oh! Oh!" gasped the little girl, as she realized her plight.

"Hold on! Hold on!" shouted Zeek. "Don't let go and you'll be all right in a minute! Hold on!"

CHAPTER XIV

BERT'S WATER MILL

NAN BOBBSEY was sure of one thing—and this was that she was going to hold with all her might to that rope attached to the hay fork. To let go, now that the fork was out of the barn and over the open yard, would mean a bad fall. So the girl clenched her fingers around the rope and set her teeth. It was a little "scary," she said afterward, to look down to the earth, though, as a matter of fact, it was not more than twenty feet below her. But that is quite a fall to take.

However, Nan's danger was soon over. The horse backed so that the laden fork and the girl came back over the wagon load of hay, and then Zeek cried:

"You can let go now! You're all right."

Nan could see this for herself. She saw that her feet dangled a little way above the big pile of hay on the wagon.

She opened her fingers and dropped into the mass of sweet-smelling grass with a sigh of relief.

"She's all right—not hurt a bit!" reported Zeek, who began climbing up to Nan as soon as he saw that she was safe. "What made you catch hold of the fork in the barn?" he asked.

"Oh, I don't know," answered the little girl, who was almost crying. "I shouldn't have done it, I know. But I saw that the hay wasn't going to drop and I had seen you pull the short rope, so I thought I could do it. But it didn't work, and before I could let go I found myself carried out of the barn."

"The hay fork prongs got jammed," explained the man in charge of unloading the wagon. "First time I've known that to happen."

Bert, who had been out in a workshop which Mr. Watson had in one of the barns, saw from Nan's face that something had happened when he noticed her walking out of the barnyard, and when he learned what it was he exclaimed:

"Jimminy, it's a good thing you held fast, Nan!"

"Yes, I knew I must do that," she said. "But what's that, Bert?" she asked, for she saw that her brother had been "making something," as he called it.

"It's going to be a water mill if I ever get it finished," he replied.

"You mean a mill to turn by water?" asked Nan.

"Yes, it's a sort of water wheel," explained Bert. "But maybe I can make it so it will turn a fan, or something like that. I'll put the wheel, with paddles on, down in the brook where there's a little waterfall," he went on. "Then I can have a belt of cord that goes around a pulley wheel on the paddles. And up at the house I can make a fan with another pulley on it. And when the water turns the paddle and pulley it will also turn the fan and we'll get a breeze on a hot day."

"Oh, that'll be fine!" cried Nan.

"It will if it works," replied Bert, more practically. "I made one last year and it didn't work. Anyhow, this one is going to be better. I'm going to try the paddle wheels now—I've got that much done. Want to come and see it work?"

"Yes," answered Nan eagerly. "I do hope it works, Bert!"

"So do I," he said.

The brook ran down at the lower end of the kitchen garden of Cloverbank. Along the bank of this stream the Bobbsey twins loved to play. The water was not deep enough, except in a few places, to make it venturesome play, and the children had been told to keep away from these spots.

"But we have to go to one of the deep spots now, to make this paddle wheel work and try my water mill," Bert said. "The only place where the water tumbles over the rocks enough to turn the paddle is where it's deep. But we'll be careful."

"Yes, we'll be careful," agreed Nan. "And Mother won't mind our going there if it's to try your mill. For she likes to be cool, and maybe she will like your fan, Bert."

"Maybe," he assented. "But I haven't got the fan part done yet—just the water mill paddle part."

As Bert and Nan made their way to a little waterfall in the brook, they heard the shouts of Flossie and Freddie, who had gone some time before to sail toy boats.

"They're having a good time," remarked Nan.

"It sounds so," agreed her brother.

But just then there was a shrill scream from Flossie, and Freddie's voice could be heard shouting:

"Oh, there he goes! Now he's in!"

Bert and Nan looked at each other with alarm. They heard a splashing of water.

"One of them has fallen in!" gasped Nan.

Guided by the shouts of the smaller twins, the older ones soon reached the place where Freddie and Flossie had been playing. As they neared the spot they heard laughter mingled with the shouts.

"I don't believe either one of them fell in," said Bert, as he slowed up a bit to wait for his sister.

"It sounded so," she said. "And we heard them say so."

Wondering what had happened to cause the splashing, the two hurried on and, pushing their way through the bushes that fringed the edge of the brook, Bert and Nan saw their brother and sister standing on the shore. But there was something in the water that excited them, for they were running up and down poking long sticks into the brook.

"What's the matter?" called Nan.

"Did anybody fall in?" Bert wanted to know.

"Just an old big bullfrog!" was Freddie's unexpected answer.

"Oh, he was such a big, fat frog!" added Flossie. "Did you hear the splash he made?"

"I should say we did!" replied Nan. "We thought maybe it was one of you."

"No," Freddie said. "But I almost fell in trying to stop the frog from getting away."

"Did you catch him? What happened?" asked Bert.

"We almost caught him," replied Freddie. "We were sailing our boats, and Flossie saw the frog. He was up on the bank, asleep in the sun."

"And Freddie said for us to get between him and the water and drive him farther up on the bank and then maybe we could catch him," added Flossie. "So we tried to creep up so he wouldn't hear us. But he has good ears, I guess, for he woke up and began to hop toward the water."

"Frogs always do that," explained Freddie, as if he knew all about such creatures. "We tried to chase him back with sticks, but he just kept on jumping this way and that way, trying to get into the brook again, and then—then——" Freddie had to stop and laugh at the memory of what had happened, so Flossie finished the story by saying:

"The big frog hopped close to Freddie and Freddie thought he could grab him and he stooped over, Freddie did, and the frog hopped right between his legs—I mean between Freddie's legs—and splashed into the brook. That's how he got away."

"Yes," added Freddie, still laughing, "that's how he got away. And I fell over, 'cause I made such a quick grab for him. But I didn't hurt myself," he added, "and I didn't get much muddy—only a little."

"I should say it was more than a little," laughed Nan. "But I guess it won't matter on your old clothes."

"No, it won't matter any," decided Freddie.

"After the frog got in," went on Flossie, "we tried to poke him out with long sticks, but he won't poke at all."

"I should think he wouldn't," chuckled

Bert. "He's glad to get away from you two. I guess he's deep down in the mud now, laughing at you."

"Well, I almost had him," was what Freddie said. Then he saw the pieces of wood Bert had and asked: "What's that— a water wheel?"

"Sort of," Bert admitted. "I'm going to try to make a water mill to run a wooden fan. I'm going down to the waterfall to try it."

"Oh, may we come?" begged Flossie.

"You may if you will promise to sit down on the bank and not come near the edge, for it's deep there!" insisted Bert.

"We'll sit down all the while. Won't we, Flossie?" asked her small brother, and she nodded her head vigorously in answer.

"Well, I guess it will be all right to take them," decided Nan.

A little later the four Bobbsey twins were at the place where the brook splashed noisily over a ledge of rocks, falling a distance of about two feet. It made a fine place to set up a water wheel, and Bert was soon fastening his in place so the falling stream would turn the paddles. If these worked he intended connecting them by means of a string belt and pulleys to a fan set up some distance away. But he had yet to build the fan.

Bert drove into the earth bank on one side of the little waterfall some pieces of wood to which he intended fastening his water mill paddle. He had finished this and was about to set up the wooden wheel when Flossie gave a startled cry.

Though he knew he had left his little sister sitting safely on the bank some distance away from the water, Bert felt that she might have gone too near the edge and might be sliding in.

"Look out!" he cried, dropping the wheel and turning around. Before he knew it, he set one foot on a slippery place on the bank. The next instant Bert felt himself sliding down toward the deep pool below the falls.

"Here I go!" he shouted wildly.

Bert could swim. Still, he did not want to fall in if he could help it, and he clutched desperately at the grassy bank.

CHAPTER XV

IN THE APPLE ORCHARD

"Bert! Bert! Hold on!" screamed Nan.

"I—I am holding on—all I can!" her brother answered.

But desperately as he clutched at the grass and ground, it was of no use. They were both wet, for Bert had splashed water around when he was working to fix his wheel in place, and farther and farther down the slope he slid.

"Oh, he'll be drowned!" yelled Flossie, as she saw what was going to happen.

"No, I won't drown!" called Bert, in reply. "But I'm going to get wet! Here I go!" he shouted, and then into the pool he plunged, going in over his head, for the falling water had washed out quite a hollow place.

"I'll get him! I'll help him out!" cried Freddie, making a dash toward his brother.

"You stay right where you are, Freddie Bobbsey!" insisted Nan, catching the little fellow before he could reach the edge of the brook. "Bert can look out for himself, and we don't want two in the water at the same time. Keep back!"

Freddie had to obey, whether he wanted to or not. But there was really no need of his help in getting Bert out, for the older lad could take good care of himself in the water.

He held his breath as he felt himself going under, and then, as he came up, as one always does after the first plunge in, he shook his head, to clear his eyes of water, and struck out for the bank, only a short distance away.

"Are you all right?" asked Nan, as he climbed out, dripping water all over like a big dog that has gone in to bring back a stick.

"Sure, I'm all right," said Bert, gasping a bit, for he had swallowed a little water. "Not hurt a bit. Only my clothes will need drying."

"I should say they would!" laughed Nan. "If you had your fan going now you could start it and stand in front of it. Wind dries clothes very fast."

"Well, I haven't got my fan, and I came

near not having my water wheel," said Bert. "I fell on it when I slipped. I hope I didn't break it."

More concerned about his latest "invention," than about himself, Bert went back to the waterfall, his shoes making a queer "sloshing" sound, as Freddie called it, for they were half full of water. He found the water wheel pulled a little out of place, for in his excitement when he found himself falling, he had made a grab for it.

"But I can easily fix that," he said, and he got a hammer, some nails and bits of wood from a box he had brought down to the brook together with his paddle wheel.

"You aren't going to keep on at that now, are you?" asked Nan, in evident surprise.

"Why not?" Bert wanted to know.

"Because you're all wet. You ought to go up to the house and get dry clothes on."

"No," said Bert. "If I go up Mother might not let me come down again. Besides, these are the oldest clothes I have and I couldn't play around again until they dried. They'll dry on me just as well as off me. I'm going to keep 'em on and stay right here."

"But you'd better take off your shoes and

stockings," Nan advised him. "They'll dry quicker off you than on you."

"I guess that's a good idea," Bert agreed, and soon his footwear was placed on bushes out in the hot sun, and he resumed work on his water mill.

Nan looked after Flossie and Freddie so they would not get in Bert's way nor into the brook, and soon the older Bobbsey boy gave a cry of delight.

"What's the matter?" Nan called.

"She works! She works!" he responded. "Look at my paddle wheel turn!"

Indeed it was splashing around bravely under the dashing water that came over the rocks. Around and around went the wooden blades, just like the larger wheel in a big mill that grinds grist for the farmers.

"Now all I have to do," said Bert, as he and the others watched how regularly the paddles turned, "is to make my fan and then connect it with this water mill by a string belt on the two pulley wheels. Then we can sit down on the porch and we'll keep cool by the fan which will be turned by this water wheel."

"Oh, Bert!" exclaimed Nan, "you can

never make the fan run so far away from the brook."

"Yes, I can," he declared. "I can have a long string belt, and it will work fine!"

But when he came to try it Bert found many difficulties in the way. True, the pulley wheel on the paddles turned around all right, and when the boy tried it with a short string belt this, too, went circling around as he held the farther end out on a smooth stick. But when he came to use a longer piece of cord, and even this was only halfway to the porch, it wouldn't turn at all.

"The reason for that," said Mrs. Bobbsey, who had, meanwhile, come to the brook, "is that your paddle wheel isn't powerful enough, Bert. It takes force to move the string, which gets wet, you see, and is all the heavier on that account. But you are wet yourself," she went on, noticing Bert's damp condition. "What happened?"

"Oh, I just—now—sort of—fell in," he admitted. "I'm all right and 'most dry. But don't you think my water wheel will turn a wooden fan up on the porch, Mother?"

"No, son, I think not," she answered. "The fan will be too far away, and the water wheel isn't powerful enough to turn the long, wet string and the fan pulley in addition. But you may try, if you like."

She knew Bert would learn best by actually doing what he had in mind, and after a day of hard work he found that his mother was right. Though the paddle wheel turned under the falling water, the long string belt would not move, and neither would the fan. Besides, the string got tangled on bushes and once Freddie reported he found a grasshopper sitting on it taking a sun bath.

"I guess I'll just work the paddle wheel in the water and nothing else," decided Bert.

"I believe that will be best," agreed his mother. "We don't really need a fan to keep cool on the porch. There are lovely cool breezes at Cloverbank."

Mr. Bobbsey returned from a trip to the city, and he and the twins and their mother had another happy day on the farm. There was so much to do and watch, aside from the gathering of the peaches, that not an hour passed without something happening, it seemed.

One afternoon when Bert and Nan decided to walk to the post-office to mail some letters and postals they had written to their play-mates in Lakeport, they passed the lower edge of the apple orchard. There they heard the voice of Flossie.

"Now look what you did, Freddie Bobb-sey!" accused the little girl. "Just look what you did! Oh, it's terrible!" and she began to cry.

"Something's happened!" shouted Bert, breaking into a run.

"Sounds so," agreed Nan. "But, anyhow, they haven't fallen into the water, for there isn't any around here."

"Maybe that calf that got all burrs and stickers is chasing them," suggested Bert. "It would be just like Freddie to try to get up on its back and ride it!"

It was nothing as exciting as this, it turned out. When Bert and Nan reached the or-chard they saw the two children standing under one of the trees, gazing up into the branches, which were laden with fruit just beginning to ripen.

"What's the matter?" asked Bert. "Is your kite up there, Freddie?"

"No! It's my doll! And Freddie threw her up there!" the little girl answered, drying her tears on her dress. "And she won't come down and maybe I'll never have her again. Oh, dear!"

"What in the world did you toss Flossie's doll up into a tree for?" asked Nan of the little boy.

"I threw her up so she'd bring down some apples," was the answer. "We wanted some apples, and we threw up stones and sticks, but we couldn't knock any down, then I asked Flossie if I shouldn't throw her doll up, 'cause she's easier to throw than a stick. Flossie said yes, so I did."

"But I didn't think my doll was going to stay up there!" objected Flossie. "You said she'd come down with some apples; that's what you did!"

"But how'd I know she was going to stick there?" asked Freddie. "Anyhow I'll climb up and get her down for you."

"No, you don't!" cried Bert, catching Freddie as he was about to climb the tree. "I see where the doll is. She's too high for you to reach. I think I can make her come down with a long stick."

Bert found one with which he managed not only to dislodge the doll, but to bring down some apples as well, to the delight of the small twins. Then, restoring her plaything to Flossie, Bert and Nan took the small ones to the post-office with them.

When they returned they heard voices in the dining room of the farmhouse—voices in excited talk, it seemed—and at the sound of one voice Bert and Nan looked at each other in surprise.

"It's Mrs. Martin!" whispered Nan.

"That's right!" agreed her brother. "I wonder if she is crazy again and has come to take the baby away?"

It was Mrs. Martin who had been left in charge of Baby Jenny while her parents went to South America and who had left the little one on the Bobbsey's doorstep in the rain that strange day. And now Mrs. Martin was at Cloverbank!

What could it mean?

CHAPTER XVI

THE RUNAWAYS

"SHALL we go in?" asked Nan of her brother in a whisper, after they had stood outside the door a few moments, listening to the voices within the room.

"Well, I guess so—yes," he replied. Then, as he listened and heard the sound of laughter mingled with the talking, he began to believe that, after all, Mrs. Martin had only called in a friendly way and not to get the baby again. "Sure, let's go in," said Bert.

Followed by Flossie and Freddie, who did not understand very much about why the other two had delayed, the twins entered the room where the old lady who had acted so strangely about "Baby May" was seated.

Mrs. Bobbsey and Mrs. Watson were also there, and so was Baby Jenny, who was being held by the old lady.

"Well, here are the lost twins!" exclaimed Mrs. Bobbsey, with a laugh, as her four entered.

"Lost! We weren't lost!" said Bert, in some surprise.

"I know—I was only joking," his mother told him. "You were gone a long time, and while you were away this friend of yours called," and she motioned to Mrs. Martin.

"Do you remember me, my dears?" asked Mrs. Martin, nodding at each of the Bobbsey twins in turn.

"Oh, yes, ma'am," answered Nan politely.

Mrs. Martin could tell that the children were just a little bit afraid of her. It really was no wonder, for she had acted very strangely in leaving Baby Jenny in a basket on the Bobbseys' steps during a storm and later stealing the baby away again. Of course afterward, as you know if you have read the book, everything came out all right.

"I am all right now," the old lady said, for she guessed that Bert and the others were looking at her curiously. "You needn't be afraid of me, my dears. I am not going to take this darling baby away any more. I just came to pay a little visit to her. But I didn't expect to find the Bobbsey twins here."

"We're glad to see you," was Bert's polite remark.

"And we're glad you're better," added Nan.

"But you look sort of—sort of different" said Freddie.

"She looks like—now—like the Grandmother in Red Riding Hood," Flossie said, after a little hesitation over the matter.

Every one laughed and Mrs. Martin said:

"It's my glasses, I guess. Always, up until a week ago, I used the kind of glasses that pinch on your nose," she told Mrs. Bobbsey and Mrs. Watson. "Then my eyes began to get worse and I went to the doctor who said I needed different glasses, and he wrote out the kind I should get on a paper.

"I took it to a shop and they made me these glasses that fasten on over my ears and stay on better than the nose kind. And I can see ever so much better. I think it must be my glasses that make me appear strange to the children."

"Yes, I guess it is," said Nan. "I never saw you with glasses on before."

"Well, I hope you will get used to them, my dear, and like me," went on Mrs. Martin. "I am quite proud of these glasses. I hope nothing happens to them," she said anxiously. "If they got broken or I lost them, I could hardly see at all, my eyes have changed so. I am getting old, I guess," she said, with a sigh. "But then we all have to do that— even Baby Jenny is older than when I so foolishly took her away and left her on your steps," she told Mrs. Bobbsey.

"Yes, and my twins are growing up, too," said their mother. "Though sometimes, when they act foolishly, fall into brooks and ride on hay forks, I fear they are growing younger instead of older," she concluded, with a laugh.

"They can't be young but once," Mrs. Martin said, as she took off her glasses to wipe them on a piece of silk she carried in her pocket. Baby Jenny had reached up and put her fingers on the glass, making a blurred place. "No, they can't be young but once —more's the pity. Have all the fun you can when you are little," she advised the children.

"I guess you don't need to tell them that," said their mother.

Flossie and Freddie went into the yard to play. Bert and Nan, after having talked a while longer with Mrs. Martin, also left the room. Later they learned that Mrs. Martin had come to stay a week or two with her cousin, Mrs. Watson.

That evening after supper the Bobbsey twins made up their minds that they were going to like Mrs. Martin very much, for she gathered them about her after the evening's play and told them some fine stories. Even Bert, who liked out-of-door games more than he did books, was interested in the tales the old lady told.

"Did somebody tell you that story?" asked Freddie, after the ending of one he had liked very much.

"No, my dear, I read it in a book," was the answer. "And now that I have my new glasses, I can read a lot more stories to tell you."

"That's good," said Flossie. "I hope nothing happens to your glasses, Mrs. Martin."

"I hope not, myself," she said. "If I lost them or broke them, I would have hard

work to replace them, especially out here
at Cloverbank. Then I couldn't read any
more."

The next day was a rainy one—the first the
children had met with since coming to Cloverbank, though, as you remember, they had
arrived in a hard shower. At first the twins
were rather disappointed when they awakened
and heard the drizzling downpour, for they
had planned a picnic in the woods. But
Mrs. Bobbsey, seeing their unhappy faces,
laughed and said:

"This is just the kind of day to play in the
attic!"

There was a bookcase in the attic, and in
it Nan found some old children's books that
had belonged to Mr. Watson's mother when
she was a little girl.

"And such funny, funny stories about such
very proper little girls I never before read,"
Nan told her mother afterward.

There were trunks full of old clothes, and
Flossie dressed up in these. There were some
ropes, too, and the boys fastened these to the
rafters and did—or Bert did and Freddie tried
to do—all sorts of acrobatic tricks. There

was old furniture, and chairs and tables were pulled out and made to do for a house, a steamboat, and a train of cars in turn.

After dinner Mrs. Watson pleaded with Mrs. Bobbsey that the boys be permitted to put on overalls and the girls old dresses and run out in the rain to play. Mrs. Bobbsey thought the children might catch cold, but Mrs. Watson laughed and said that such a warm summer rain would never hurt running children, if they came in and dried themselves as soon as they stopped playing.

So out in the falling rain rushed Nan and Bert, Freddie and Flossie, and such a game of tag as they had, the smaller twins not always being caught, either! Then came a jolly game of puss-wants-a-corner, with trees for corners. After this they went in the house again and, after putting on dry clothing, went back to the attic for the rest of the afternoon.

Before the Bobbsey twins knew it the rainy day had passed and night had come. They had spent many happy hours in the attic, and running about in the rain. Then came an evening story by Mrs. Martin, and soon it was bedtime, even for the older twins, Bert and Nan.

"Well, I'm glad to see the sun," said Mr. Watson the next morning after breakfast. "I was afraid it was going to rain and I couldn't get the rest of my peaches picked. But this is a fine day."

As soon as the orchard had dried up a little, the men and women peach-gatherers appeared, and soon there were the same busy scenes that the visitors had observed when they first came to Cloverbank.

As more pickers came to work than he expected, Mr. Watson soon found that a great quantity of fruit was gathered in the barn to be sorted, and this must be done quickly, so the baskets could be hurried to the market to be sold.

"I'll come out and help you sort," offered Mr. Bobbsey, who had returned from his trip to the city.

"So will I," his wife said.

"We will, too!" exclaimed Nan and Bert.

The small twins offered their services, but as it was doubtful whether or not they could tell choice fruit from that intended for the near-by canning factory, their mother decided they had better play about the barn while the others sorted.

The barn was soon a busy place, with the small truck and wagon bringing in the fruit from the orchard, and the sorters picking out the different grades. The whole place had a most delightful perfume about it from the crushed peaches, for, in spite of care, some would fall and be bruised, quickly getting soft.

Bert and Nan soon learned to do good work at the sorting bins, watching what the expert workers did, and Mr. Watson, pausing near them once or twice, said they were doing very well. Mrs. Bobbsey, knowing a lot about peaches, for she had canned many of them, was able to work with the best of them. Nor was Mr. Bobbsey far behind.

"I'm glad you Bobbsey folks came out to Cloverbank," chuckled the farmer, during a lull in the work. "I never had such a big crop of peaches before, and good workers are scarce."

"We're working for our board," Mrs. Bobbsey said, with a laugh. "And that reminds me, Mr. Watson! Your wife said she would like you to send a few baskets of peaches to the house, as some friends of hers are going to stop for them during the day."

"I'll have Zeek take out some ripe ones," was the answer, and this was done, the baskets of peaches being set on the porch of the farmhouse.

It was just before noon, and Bert and Nan were having a race to see who could sort the most peaches, when suddenly there arose a great shouting outside the barn.

"What's that?" exclaimed Mrs. Bobbsey.

"Maybe somebody else upset a load of peaches," suggested Bert.

But Freddie, who was near the open door of the barn, began to dance in excitement at something he saw.

"They're running away! Oh, look at the runaways!" he cried.

"Are the horses running away?" asked his father, for Mr. Watson was using a team to haul wagonloads of peaches in from the orchard.

"No, it isn't horses! It's cows! A lot of cows running away! They're coming right into the barn, too! Oh, look!"

CHAPTER XVII

MRS. MARTIN'S GLASSES

FOR a moment or two, following Freddie's excited cries, those in the barn, including the others in the Bobbsey family, did not know whether the little fellow really saw what he said he did or not.

"What do you mean, Freddie—are there really runaway cows?" asked Nan.

"Sure, they are!" was the answer. "Come and look! They're running right this way, too!"

"And I can hear cows, too!" shrieked Flossie.

"I'll see what's going on!" exclaimed Zeek Trimmer from his place at the far end of the peach bins, where he was putting the fruit into baskets ready for the market.

He ran to the door, followed by Mr. Watson and Mr. Bobbsey. Freddie had turned to find what he thought would be a safe place with Flossie. Nan decided she must help her mother quiet the small twins, but Bert ran on with his father and the other men.

Flossie was right when she said she could hear the cows, for loud bellows and moos filled the air, mingling with the shouts of men.

Bert looked out in time to see a large herd of cattle rushing up the lane that led from the main road to the biggest of the Cloverbank barns. The animals seemed to have been frightened by something, and were now running away, or "stampeding," as a Western cowboy would have called it.

"Where'd they come from?" asked Mr. Bobbsey. "Are they your cattle, Mr. Watson?"

"No, they don't belong to me. I haven't as many as that. They must be a herd some drover was driving to market, and they got wild for some reason or other."

"Well, if we don't shut these doors they'll be in the barn in another minute!" cried Zeek. "And if they knock over the peach baskets and bins and trample the fruit, there'll be a big loss. Help me close the doors!" he shouted.

"That's a good idea!" exclaimed Mr. Bobbsey, and while some of the peach sorters ran out to help the drover and his men quiet the runaway cattle, others began closing the big doors of the barn.

By this time the excited cattle were all about the building, running this way and that, kicking up their heels, shaking their horned heads, and acting wildly.

"They'll break down my fences and let out my cattle if we don't drive them away!" said Mr. Watson, when he, with Mr. Bobbsey and the other men, had gone outside, after closing the doors to save the peaches.

"Help me get 'em back into the road and they'll be all right!" shouted a man with a long whip. He evidently was in charge of the herd, and had two other men to help. "Drive 'em back into the road!" he cried.

"What happened?" Mr. Watson wanted to know.

"Dogs and bees!" was the answer. "A stray dog started one of the heifers off on a run. She got in among some bee hives down the road and kicked over some of the hives. The bees swarmed out and stung a lot of the cows, and they got wild and started to run. Then the whole bunch started off!"

"We'll help you get them back into shape again," said Mr. Bobbsey.

"Can't I come?" asked Bert, who was eager to do his part.

"Yes, come along!" invited Mr. Watson.

"This is fun!" exulted Bert, as he caught up a stick to wave at the cows and get them back on the main highway.

It may have been fun for Bert Bobbsey, but it was worrisome work for the drover and his men. But finally the bunch of runaway cattle were rounded up, and they were slowly driven out of the lane, away from the peach barn, and toward the main road. Some of Mr. Watson's cattle, in a near-by pasture, seeing the other bunch of animals, seemed to want to join them. They ran excitedly up and down the field, as close to the fence as they could get.

"If they break out you'll have hard work separating your cows from the others," said Mr. Bobbsey to the farmer.

"I guess they won't break out," was the reply. "My fences are good and strong."

It was well they were, for some of the cows tried to knock the rails down with their heads and horns. But the barriers held, and when the runaway cattle were driven back to the highway, the Cloverbank cows quieted down.

Bert did good work, running here and there after stray animals and preventing them from turning back up the lane again. The cows did not seem to know what to do nor where to go.

"Bees and a barking dog are a bad combination in a herd of cattle," remarked Mr. Watson, when the drover was thanking him for having helped to get the animals started on their way again. "It's a good thing your animals didn't overrun my farm."

"Yes, I'm glad they didn't do any damage," said the other. "Though I would have been willing to pay for it if they had."

"I mean I'm glad they didn't get among my bee hives," went on Mr. Watson. "A second stinging would have made them wilder than ever."

"I guess it would!" agreed the drover. "But I don't see any hives around here," he added.

This was the first Bert knew honey was produced on the farm.

"Yes, I have quite a few swarms of bees," replied Mr. Watson. "They're over in that valley," and he pointed to a distant one the children had not yet visited. "There's lots of clover around here, and clover blossoms make the best honey," he said. "Though some folks like the strong black honey made from buckwheat blossoms, and some say basswood honey is good. But clover suits me."

"Was anybody hurt?" called Mrs. Watson to her husband. She stood on the side porch of the house, holding Baby Jenny, and with her was Mrs. Martin.

"Nobody hurt," her husband answered. "Did any of the cattle get up around the house?" he asked, for he had been so busy driving away those near the barn that he had noticed little else.

"There were a few up here," Mrs. Martin said. "They acted just like they wanted to come into the house."

"Maybe they wanted to give some milk to the baby," suggested Freddie.

"Well, they didn't get a chance!" cried the old lady. "I caught up the broom and drove 'em away. Then they headed for the garden, and I had to go after 'em again!"

"You must have had quite a time up here," said Mr. Bobbsey.

"We did," Mrs. Watson said. "For a little while I thought surely some of the cows would come into the house. What happened?"

She was told about the bees and the dog.

What might have been a serious matter passed away safely, though the runaway cattle were the cause of something happening a little later to Mrs. Martin.

The stampede had interrupted the peach sorting, but no damage had been done, and Mr. Watson said Freddie had been a "brave little scout," to warn so quickly about the danger of the onrushing cattle.

"If they'd once got into the barn here, among my fruit, they would have done a lot of damage," the farmer said. "You are quite a cowboy, Freddie!"

"No, I'm going to be a fireman when I grow up," was the answer. "Once I was going to be a cowboy, but my sister Flossie doesn't like cows, so I'm going to be a fireman, and she can come and see me put out fires."

"I didn't know you kept bees, Mr. Watson," said Nan, when quiet was once more restored in the barn.

"Oh, yes," he said. "I bought some from a man who didn't make much of a success producing honey for the market. I left the bees over where he had them—that's the reason you've never seen the hives around here."

"Will there be some honey soon?" asked Freddie.

"I shouldn't wonder but what there would," was the answer. "Anyhow, there will be plenty in the fall, and I'll see that you get some to eat on your pancakes this winter. I'll send you some."

"I like pancakes!" murmured Freddie.

Knowing that too much work would not please the children, Mr. Bobbsey suggested that they had been in the barn long enough, sorting peaches, and told them to run out and play.

This Flossie and Freddie did, going to their favorite place down by the shallow part of the brook, where they sailed tiny boats. Bert and Nan, after having really helped quite a bit in sorting the fruit, wandered off to the woods, Nan taking a story book.

Bert decided he would go fishing.

"Want to come, Nan?" he invited, for he liked to have his sister with him.

"Thank you, I guess I don't," she answered. "I'll take my book back to the house and read in the hammock."

Bert went back to the house with her to get his pole and line. When they arrived they saw Mrs. Martin excitedly walking about the porch, looking on window sills, under chairs, and in many places.

"What's the matter?" asked Nan.

"Is the baby lost?" Bert wanted to know.

"Not the baby, but my glasses!" answered the old lady. "Oh, dear! I had them just before the runaway cattle appeared, and I must have taken them off and laid them some place. Now I can't find them! And I've gotten so used to them I don't know what to do without them! Oh, where are my glasses?" and she seemed much distressed over the loss.

CHAPTER XVIII

THE QUEER CLOUD

"We'll help you look for your glasses, Mrs. Martin," offered Nan, though she wished very much to finish her story. "Won't we, Bert?"

"Sure, we will," he answered, boy-fashion. And, though he very much wanted to go fishing, he gave up his pleasure for the time being to help the old lady.

Mrs. Martin was really quite distressed about losing her glasses, as most people are whose eyes are so poor that they cannot see well nor read without the help of spectacles.

"Where did you have them last?" asked Nan, as she had often heard her mother ask when one of the children lost a toy.

"I had them on my head, over my nose, and in front of my eyes," Mrs. Martin answered. "Then, all of a sudden, I heard

Mrs. Watson cry out about the cattle coming into the garden, and I grabbed off my glasses to get the broom. I was afraid I'd break them chasing after the cows."

By this time Mrs. Watson, who had been putting the baby to sleep, came out on the side porch.

"Yes, I saw your glasses on you just before the cattle began running wild," said Jenny's mother. "Then so much happened all at once that I don't know what you did with them."

"Maybe they're still up on top of your head," suggested Bert. "Once Charlie Mason's grandmother lost her glasses and we looked all over for them, and, all the while, she had them pushed up on top of her head."

"Well, mine aren't there," Mrs. Martin replied, putting up her hand, however, to feel and make sure. "I don't see what I did with them!"

Then the search began, with the older Bobbsey twins and Mrs. Watson helping. The porch was searched carefully, and the children looked on the ground around it, stepping carefully so they would not tread on and break the glasses if they should have happened to fall. But the glasses could not be found.

Then Mrs. Bobbsey came and helped, but she was no more successful than the others had been. Inside and outside the house the search went on, but the spectacles could not be found.

"Maybe they'll turn up after a while," said Mr. Watson, when he came in from the peach sorting to get washed for dinner.

"Well, I hope they will," his wife's cousin said. "Meanwhile I can't read a word, and I can't see very well. I declare, I can hardly tell one Bobbsey twin from the other!" she said with a sigh.

"We can tell you our names," Freddie suggested. He and Flossie had come back from sailing their toy boats and had taken part in the hunt for the glasses.

"Yes, my dear, that's kind of you, and I suppose you could do that," murmured the old lady. "But I would like to see."

When a further search did not bring the missing glasses to light Mr. Watson said:

"Can't you mail the prescription to the people who made them and have another set made?"

"Yes, I could do that if I had the prescription," agreed Mrs. Martin. "But I haven't got that paper. I lost it. If I only had it things wouldn't be so bad, for it would mean only a few days before I could order new spectacles by mail. But I've lost the prescription."

"Your doctor has a copy," Mr. Watson said. "Eye doctors always keep copies of the prescriptions they give their patients."

"Probably Dr. Bangert has a copy of mine," Mrs. Martin agreed, with a sigh. "But he has gone away on his summer vacation and I don't know where to reach him. When he gave me the perscription he told me to take good care of it, as he was going away and could not be reached until the fall. I think he has gone hunting in the wilds of Canada."

"Then it looks as if you would either have to go to another doctor around here and get him to fit you with glasses," said Mr. Watson, "or else find those that are lost."

"I don't want to go to another doctor," said Mrs. Martin. "I don't believe anybody but Dr. Bangert could fit my eyes. Oh, I must find those glasses! They can't be far away."

"Maybe they got caught on one of the horns of the cows and carried off," suggested Freddie.

"You think of the funniest things!" laughed Mrs. Watson. "But the cows didn't come near enough the porch to take my cousin's glasses. She must have dropped them in some out-of-the-way corner."

Though once again they searched all over, even in places where Mrs. Martin said she had never been with her glasses, the spectacles could not be found and she was quite in despair.

Having done all he could to help the old lady, Bert decided that he would spend the afternoon fishing, for he was fond of this sport and Mr. Watson had said that in a creek across the meadow from the brook there were good fish to be had.

He had brought his fishing outfit with him, so that all he needed now was some bait, and n the advice of Zeek he took both worms and grasshoppers. The worms he and his brother and Nan dug in the garden, putting the crawling creatures in a baking-powder box, with some earth. To give the worms air Bert punched holes in the top and bottom of the tin box.

"Sometimes when the fish won't bite on worms they will on grasshoppers," suggested the hired man. "Just take another box with you and walk through the lower hay meadow. The grasshoppers are thick there. You can catch them in your hand as you walk along and pop them in the box. But you want to be careful how you do it."

"Why, will grasshoppers bite?" asked Bert, though he had never heard of them doing that.

"No," answered the hired man, with a laugh. "But after you catch one grasshopper and put it in the box, when you take off the cover to put in another, often the first one will jump out. And you can't catch many fish on one hopper."

"Oh, I see what you mean," laughed Bert.

He found it just as Zeek had said. It was easy enough to grab a green grasshopper off a head of timothy grass in the hay field, but when he caught his second one and opened the box cover to slip the creature in, out jumped the first one.

But Bert made a prisoner of the second one, and when he had his third he was more careful in opening the box. He raised the lid only a little way, and through the crack he shoved the green insect. Soon he had enough, he thought, with the worms he had brought, and he made his way to the edge of the creek, picking out a spot where the water foamed and bubbled over the stony bottom.

As worms were easier to put on the hook than the grasshoppers, which were very lively, Bert baited with one of the crawling creatures and cast in his hook. The Bobbsey boy was about as patient as most lads, but when he had pulled out several times, thinking he had bites, and found nothing on his hook, Bert began to think perhaps it would be well to change the bait.

He opened his other tin box to get one of the grasshoppers, but no sooner was the lid raised than, with one accord, every grasshopper in the container leaped out and sailed away.

"Well—say—that wasn't very polite!" laughed Bert. "Still, I can't blame you!" he went on. "I guess it isn't much fun to be stuck on a hook and swallowed by a fish. I'll catch my grasshoppers right here, one at a time, as I need them," he said.

He had noticed that in the field just back of

the place he had picked out for fishing, many grasshoppers were jumping from weed to weed. Bert laid aside his pole, having noted that the worm had been nearly nibbled off the hook now by small fish, too little to land, and, going back, he caught a grasshopper in his hand.

"Now for a big fish!" said the lad.

But after waiting some time and getting no bites, Bert was inclined to think that he had chosen a wrong spot or else that his bait or the day was wrong. His first guess was borne out a little later when a voice hailed him, saying:

"You'll never get any fish there!"

Bert Bobbsey turned and saw a country lad of about his own age standing on the edge of the weed-grown field. The boy was bare-footed, his clothes were ragged, and he had a torn straw hat on his head. Over his shoulder was a crooked stick cut from a tree, and fastened to it was a line with many knots in it, as if it had been broken and tied a number of times.

"Why won't I get any fish here?" asked Bert.

" 'Cause there aren't any there—it's too

shallow. If you want to get big ones you'll have to go up above to the eddy, where the water's deep."

"Well, I must say I haven't had much luck here," admitted Bert. "I've tried worms and grasshoppers, and the only bites are little nibbles."

"Those are just baby fish. They suck off the bait without getting caught on the hook," said the country lad. "Come on with me if you want to, and I'll show you a good place."

"Thanks," answered Bert. "Do you live around here?"

"Yes, just over that hill. My name's Sam Porter. What's yours?"

"Bert Bobbsey," was the answer.

"You live around here?" asked Sam. "I never saw you before that I know of."

"No, I don't live here," Bert said. "I'm visiting at Cloverbank."

"Oh, yes, I know Mr. Watson!" exclaimed Sam. "My father works for him. He's picking peaches now."

Sam proved to be a nice lad, and he and Bert soon became good friends, talking about fishing and other outdoor sports. Sam led the way up the bank of the creek to a quiet, shady spot beneath some overhanging willow trees.

"There's the eddy," he said, pointing to where the water ran deep and quiet. The stream had washed out a place in the earth bank, making a deep pool where the water swirled around in a circle, or "eddy," as the country lad called it. On the other side of the creek, opposite this point, the stream was shallow and ran rapidly over the stones.

"But the big fish come to this pool," Sam said. "You'll soon have a big one!"

He was right. Bert had only thrown his worm-baited hook in the water and waited a few minutes before the bobber on his line dipped suddenly under water.

"You've got him! A big one!" whispered Sam. "Pull up!"

Neither Sam nor Bert were doing fishing in a scientific way with a reel, and the only way to land a fish, once he was hooked, was to pull up the pole quickly.

This Bert Bobbsey did. He felt a weight on his bamboo rod, and as it went in a sweeping circle over his head he had a glimpse of something flashing like silver in the sun.

"You got him! A beauty!" yelled Sam. "A big one!"

When Bert ran to look in the grass, where he had landed his catch, he was delighted to find that he had caught a good-sized chub, as Sam named the fish.

"Say, you brought me to a good place all right!" cried Bert in delight to his companion. "There's fish here all right! I hope you get one!"

"Oh, I'll get one all right," said Sam. "I hardly ever come here without getting as many as we can use at home. My mother likes fish, and about twice a week I come here to get a mess."

He had retained his seat on the bank, his line dangling in the water, while Bert landed his catch, and he watched the Bobbsey boy as he took the chub off the hook—which was not easy to do, since the fish had swallowed the hook in its eagerness to get the bait. When Bert had his prize loose, he strung a string through the gills and then, fastening on a cross-stick so the fish would not slip off, he put it back in a little pool, tying the shore end of the string to a tree.

The chub feebly flapped its tail and tried

to swim away, but he was held a prisoner. In the water he would be kept fresh until Bert was ready to go home with any others he might land.

Sam caught the next one, tossing back on the grass a fish not quite as big as Bert's, but fair in size.

"Now my luck's beginning!" exclaimed Sam, as he fastened his fish to another string and let it swim about in a pool. His fish had only been hooked through the lip and was hardly hurt at all.

The two lads then "took turns," so to speak, in landing fish. It was a fine day and a good place, and first Bert would land one and then Sam would follow.

"Well, I guess I have enough," Bert said, after a while.

"And I have, too," agreed Sam. "We might as well clean 'em and wash 'em here and then there won't be such a mess around the house."

The boys prepared the fish for cooking and then put them with wet grass in baskets they had brought for that purpose.

"If you come with me across this field, I'll show you a short cut back to Cloverbank," suggested Sam, when they were ready to go.

"All right."

The two boys were going across a green meadow in a little valley between two low hills, when Bert suddenly heard a low, humming sound in the air. At first he thought it was a distant aeroplane, but on looking around he saw what seemed to be a small black cloud coming toward him and Sam.

"Look!" cried Bert, pointing.

"Golly! We'd better duck!" exclaimed Sam.

He dropped his pole and basket of fish and began running toward a low clump of bushes, calling to Bert as he ran:

"Come on! Come on in here until it gets past!"

CHAPTER XIX

HIVING THE BEES

Bert Bobbsey did not understand what Sam Porter's excitement was all about. But he could tell, by the way Sam acted and by the way he called, that it was something serious. So he dropped his fish and his pole and made ready to follow his new chum.

"Come on! Come on!" called Sam, peering out from his shelter in the bushes, as he saw that Bert was not hurrying as much as he might. "Run for it, if you don't want to get stung!"

"Stung!" exclaimed Bert.

"Yep," answered the country lad. "Don't you see? That's a bunch of bees with the queen bee in the middle, and they're looking for a place to settle so they can start a new home. I only hope they don't 'light on this bush," he added, as Bert crawled in the shelter with him. "If they do—oh, boy!

Look out for yourself! The best thing to do
will be to leg it for the creek and jump in.
Just let your nose stick out—that's all! I
hope they don't decide to settle here where
we are!"

But the swarm of humming, busy little insects, following their queen, suddenly turned
and made for a tree not far away. There
the bees clustered in a bunch on one of the
low branches.

"That's good!" cried Sam. "Mr. Watson
can easily get them from there. Come on,
we'll go tell him!"

The boys picked up their fish and their
poles, and soon they were at Cloverbank.

"Oh, what a fine lot of fish!" exclaimed
Mrs. Bobbsey as she saw the two boys with
their strings.

"Yes, they're good fish," Bert said. "But
will you take them, please, Nan. I have to
go with Sam and tell Mr. Watson about his
swarm of bees."

"What's this about the bees?" Mrs. Bobbsey wanted to know.' The boys, taking
turns, quickly told her, and Bert added:

"I'm going to watch Mr. Watson catch
them."

"Oh, so am I!" cried Freddie.

Nan hurried back to the farmhouse with the two strings of fish, which were to be put in the cool cellar until needed. Sam said he would come back and get his after the bees were caught.

"So some of my bees got away, did they?" asked Mr. Watson when he had been told the news. He was about to set out for another of his orchards where peaches were being picked, but when he heard about his honey-makers he decided to postpone his orchard trip.

Followed by the Bobbsey twins, their mother and Sam, Mr. Watson hurried to the little valley where he kept about a hundred hives of bees. Like little dog-houses the hives were, only with flat instead of peaked roofs, and of course only a small slit was needed in the bottom of each hive-house to let the bees fly in and out. The hives stood in rows in an orchard of apple trees near a small garden. There was a farmhouse in this valley in which lived a man and his wife who looked after the bees.

"I had three swarms out to-day," called Jason Stern, the bee-keeper, to Mr. Watson when the latter arrived. "I couldn't get them all. One got away."

"I know where it is," the peach-grower answered. "Bert and Sam saw the swarm alight when they were coming back from fishing. I'll take an empty hive on the small hand-cart and bring them back. You'd better come along to help—that is, if you have the other swarms safe."

"Yes, they're all right except the one that got away," said Mr. Stern.

While the Bobbsey twins watched, Mr. Watson and the bee-keeper put rubber gloves on their hands and on their heads big straw hats, the brim of which held the mosquito netting veil away from their faces so no bee could get near them. They also tied down the legs of their trousers.

"For sometimes a bee or two will crawl up your pants, and it isn't very pleasant," said Jason Stern, with a laugh.

Then a two-wheeled cart with a flat wooden platform was brought out of the barn and the party set off.

They presently came in view of the tree on which the swarm had alighted. The cluster of bees was like a big football, and somewhat similar in shape. A low, buzzing sound could be heard.

"Better not come any closer with the children," advised the farmer to Mrs. Bobbsey. "A stray bee or two might sting them. You can watch Jason and me from here."

The mother of the twins, and in fact the twins themselves, as well as Sam, did not care to go too near. So they sat down on a grassy hillock while the two men wheeled the cart close under the tree. On the cart was an empty beehive, one of many kept ready for just such occasions as this. Also, Mr. Stern had brought with him a "smoker," which was something like a tin funnel with a little leather bellows beneath it. When this bellows was pumped, clouds of smoke were sent out of the small end of the funnel. Directed against the swarm of bees, the smoke quieted them so they would not sting those who handled them.

The cart, with the open empty hive on it, was wheeled up until it was directly under the branch on which hung the clustering bees around their queen.

"You hold the cart steady now, Jason," directed Mr. Watson, "and I'll climb up in the tree and jar them off. As soon as most of them are inside the hive, clap the cover on."

"All right," was the answer.

"I wonder what would happen," said Bert, "if the cluster of bees and their queen should fall on Mr. Stern's head instead of in the empty hive."

"It wouldn't be very pleasant," his mother answered. "Though I guess, with the veils, the men won't get stung. But watch now, children, and see them hive the runaway bees."

"Jason, are you all ready down there?" called Mr. Watson to his bee-man, when the farmer himself was up in the tree.

"All ready," was the answer. "Shake 'em down!"

CHAPTER XX

THE PIRATE'S CAVE

WHILE the Bobbsey twins and Sam, standing near Mrs. Bobbsey, watched, the peach-grower suddenly jarred the branch on which had gathered the runaway bees, clustered about their queen like faithful subjects. Down dropped the buzzing brown mass of honey-gatherers into the open hive box.

"You got most of 'em!" shouted Jason Stern, as, with a quick motion, he clapped the cover on the hive and started drawing the cart away.

"Won't the bees get out the little front door?" asked Flossie, for she had noticed that the hive box had a slit at the bottom.

"I stopped that up before I put the hive on the cart," said Mr. Stern. "The bees are safely caged now—that is all but a few that got away."

The children could see a few of the insects, which had not fallen into the hive, flying around the tree and around the white box that now contained the queen and thousands of workers. Perhaps these stray bees were wondering where their monarch had disappeared to.

"Don't wheel your cart over toward the children," warned Mr. Watson, as he climbed down out of the tree. "Some of the stray bees may sting them."

"I'll be careful," said the bee-man. He puffed into the air around the hive some smoke from the smoker, and this served to drive away the humming bees that, after circling about for a while, flew off in the direction of the orchard.

"They'll go back to the old hive," Mr. Watson said, as he took off his veil and gloves, for there was no longer need of them. "And the bees and the queen in this new hive will start making the wax cells into which they will put honey a little later. I'm glad you saw this swarm and came to tell me, boys," he said to Sam and Bert. "It's worth quite a few dollars, or will be this fall when the hive is filled with honey."

"I like honey," remarked Freddie, looking carefully at Mr. Watson to make sure no bees had followed him. But none had.

"Well, I'll send you some when you get back home," promised the peach-grower.

"That was very interesting," said Mrs. Bobbsey as she turned to take the path across the fields to Cloverbank. "Bees are very smart little creatures."

"And they'll make you smart if they sting you!" said Bert.

"Oh, that's a good joke!" exclaimed Nan, with a laugh. "I'm going to put that in my composition."

"You can put in about your brother catching a big fish, too," said Sam. "He got the biggest one of the lot."

"Oh, did you?" cried Nan. "I'm glad of that. And I can write about it. Oh, I do hope I win that prize!" she went on.

"I hate to write compositions," declared Sam to Bert. "Don't you?"

"I sure do," was the answer. "I'd rather go fishing any day!"

From a safe distance, when they had gone back to the little bee-farm, the children watched the hive of runaways and their captive queen set down amid the rows of other busy insects. The piece of wood that had blocked the "front door" was taken away and soon the members of the new colony of honey-gatherers were flying out and in.

Then Mr. Stern brought out some honey, from the crop of the previous season, and gave the Bobbsey twins and Sam a treat.

"Lots has happened to-day," remarked Bert, when Sam had gone home after getting his string of fish from the cellar and the children were sitting on the porch of the farm-house, waiting for the evening meal, which was almost ready.

"I'm glad of it," announced Nan, who was writing with an old, big geography book on her knees. "I'm making a list of the different things," she went on, "and I'm going to put the best of them in my composition. Tell me how you felt, Bert, when you pulled out the big fish."

"Oh, I felt fine!" he answered, with a laugh.

"I wish I could catch a fish," sighed Freddie. "I'm kind of tired playing with my fire engine."

"I'll take you fishing to-morrow," promised Bert. "I know a dandy place now. Sam showed me."

"I wouldn't go to-morrow," said Mrs. Bobbsey.

"Why not?" Bert wanted to know.

"Because that's the day Daddy promised to take you to the woods for a picnic."

"Oh, so it is!" cried Bert. "I forgot about that. We'll go fishing some other time, Freddie."

"All right," agreed the little boy. "Picnics are just as nice as fish."

"Nicer, I think," Flossie said. "'Cause you can eat at picnics and you can't eat fish!"

"Sure, you can eat fish!" exclaimed Bert. "What did I catch 'em for if they aren't to be eaten?"

"Well, I don't like to eat fish," Flossie went on; "so I'd rather have a picnic."

"We'll go to-morrow," promised her mother.

Mrs. Martin came out on the porch, looking from side to side anxiously.

"Have you found your glasses yet?" asked Nan.

"No, dearie, I haven't," was the answer. "And I feel quite lost without them. I can't read a word. You children haven't seen them anywhere, have you?"

None of the Bobbseys had, though, led by Nan, Flossie and Freddie gave another search about the house and the side porch. But the old lady's glasses seemed to have vanished completely, and she did not know what to do about getting another pair.

"I guess I'll just have to wait until my doctor comes back in the fall," she said, with a sigh.

The next day proved to be a bright and sunshiny one—just the best kind for a picnic.

Mrs. Watson decided to take Baby Jenny with them on the outing, and soon after breakfast she and the little one joined the Bobbsey family in Mr. Bobbsey's auto. They were to go to a glen about ten miles away, there to spend the day. In the glen, or little valley between two high, rocky places, was a waterfall, much larger than the one in the brook where Bert had placed his wooden mill.

"I wish I had made a bigger paddle wheel so I could fasten it under the big waterfall we are going to see," said Bert, when they were almost ready to start.

"It would have to be a big paddle, for there is quite a fall in Buttermilk Glen," Mrs. Watson said, with a laugh.

"Why do they call it that?" asked Nan.

"Because some one thought the water, falling over the ledge of rocks, looked like buttermilk, I suppose," was the answer. "Do you want to go to Nan?" the mother asked Baby Jenny who was holding out her hands toward Bert's twin sister. "Well, I guess you may." So, to her delight, Nan was allowed to hold the baby during part of the auto ride to Buttermilk Glen.

Baskets of food had been packed, for the picnic was to last all day and they would eat in the woods, the prospect of which gave the twins joy and delight.

"We'll have more peaches picked ready for you to sort when you get back," Mr. Watson called to the picnic party as they drove away. "I never had such a big crop."

"We'll help you to-morrow," promised Bert.

Buttermilk Glen was soon reached. It was a picnic ground well known for miles around, though when those from Cloverbank arrived they had the place to themselves.

"I hear the waterfall!" cried Freddie as soon as they alighted from the auto at the entrance to the glen. The road was too rough to drive all the way up into the place.

"Yes, that's it," said Mrs. Watson. "It's very pretty when the water is high; and in winter, when it freezes, it is even more beautiful. But I know some one who is sleepy!" she went on in a singing voice.

"I'm not!" quickly cried Flossie. "I didn't come here to sleep."

"She means Jenny," whispered Nan, and, sure enough, the little one's head was nodding and her eyes were closing. Her mother wrapped Jenny in a blanket and put her down under a tree, while Mr. Bobbsey got out the lunch baskets and the Bobbsey twins scattered here and there to play.

"You may have fun for about two hours, and then we'll eat," said Mrs. Bobbsey. "After lunch you may play about some more before we start for home."

With shouts of delight the boys and girls began exploring the picnic ground. They had never been there before, and there was much to see and admire.

"We'll climb up the sides and get to the top of the waterfall after lunch," Bert decided. "Maybe I can fish up there. It's a big fall—too big for my little paddle wheel in the brook. But maybe I could make a big wheel that would turn here."

A path led up one side of the cliff a little distance below the fall, and up this, Mrs. Watson said, the children could make their way to the top of the fall.

But there was plenty to see down below, and what with exploring, finding pretty stones, and wading barefooted in little pools, the four had lots of fun.

After a time Bert and Freddie found themselves some distance up in the glen, which divided into two parts—one where the stream ran down the center, and another part where it was dry. Flossie and Nan had gone back to their mother and father, who sat talking with Mrs. Watson.

"Look, there's a cave!" suddenly exclaimed Freddie, pointing to a dark opening in the rocky side of the gorge.

"So it is!" agreed Bert. "A regular pirate's cave, I'll say! Let's go in!"

Freddie hesitated a moment. The place looked dark and not very inviting.

"Oh, I don't guess I want to," Freddie said.

"Well, I'm going in," Bert declared. "I want to see what's there. Nothing can hurt you," he went on. "Even if a pirate was there once he's gone now."

"You go in first, and then maybe I will," Freddie suggested. So Bert disappeared into the blackness. Freddie was just going to ask if everything was all right when Bert suddenly shouted:

"Oh! Oh! I'm falling! Oh, Freddie!"

Then the older boy's voice died away and Freddie was left alone, outside the pirate's cave.

CHAPTER XXI

FLOSSIE'S TARTS

FREDDIE BOBBSEY was a resourceful little lad for his age. It was not the first time he and Bert had gone exploring together, nor the first time something had happened. So now, instead of rushing into the small cave after his brother, as many boys or girls might have done, Freddie turned to hurry back to his father and mother.

"I'll go and get somebody to help you, Bert!" he called. "Maybe if I went in I'd fall too, 'cause it looks dark! I'll get help!"

Bert did not answer, and this made Freddie fear lest something serious had happened. But even then he knew the best thing to do was to bring help as quickly as possible.

Back he hurried to the others, running all the way. Mrs. Bobbsey could tell by the look on her small son's face and by his

224

manner that something unusual had taken place.

"Where's Bert?" she quickly asked, for she remembered that the two boys had gone into the deeper part of Buttermilk Glen together.

"He's in the pirate's cave!" answered Freddie, panting for breath. "He hollered something about falling down and then he didn't holler any more and I came back to tell you!"

Instantly there was great excitement.

"In the pirate's cave!"

"Is he lost?" Flossie wanted to know.

"You did right to come back so quickly and tell us," Mr. Bobbsey said. "Do you know where this cave is?" he asked Mrs. Watson.

"Yes, I know of a cave," she answered. "It isn't a very large place, nor is it dangerous. I can't understand about Bert's falling. There are no holes in the place that I know of, though I haven't been in it for years."

"Maybe he stumbled over a ledge and fell, striking his head," suggested Mr. Bobbsey, as he jumped up and went to his coat which was hanging on a tree near by. He took some matches from one of the pockets. "I'll make a bark torch to go into the cave and find Bert," he said to his wife. "I didn't bring the flashlight. Can you show me where the cave is, Freddie?"

"I can lead you to the cave," said Mrs. Watson, noticing that Baby Jenny was still peacefully sleeping. "Nan, you and Flossie stay here with her, and your mother and I will go with your father and Freddie to the cave."

Nan and Flossie would have liked to go, too, to search for Bert, but they said nothing as they watched the others start.

It did not take them long to reach the place. Mrs. Watson had often been to the glen on picnics and she knew all its windings and turns. Soon they stood in front of the small cavern which Bert, in common with other boys, had named "pirate's cave."

"Bert! Bert! Are you all right?" his mother called. But still there was no answer.

"He didn't speak to me, after he hollered about falling," reported Freddie.

"He must be in a faint, after falling and hitting his head," suggested Mr. Bobbsey. "I'll go in with the torch and see."

"I'm coming, too!" insisted Mrs. Bobbsey, while Mrs. Watson said she would stay outside with Freddie.

Bert's father pulled off some dry bark, and, twisting it into a torch, set fire to it. This gave him and his wife light enough to see, though rather dimly, as they entered the small cavern. It was just about high enough to stand upright in, and seemed to be a cave that had been hollowed out by the washing of high water in the glen.

Holding the torch before him, Mr. Bobbsey went inside, followed by his wife. He had taken only a few steps before he suddenly cried:

"Stop! Don't come any farther! There's a hole here, and you may tumble in!"

"Is Bert there?" asked Mrs. Bobbsey. Her husband flashed the torch down and as far ahead of him as he could, and then he said:

"Yes, he's here! And he seems to be all right, too. He's moving. I guess he was dazed by the blow on his head. Hold the torch, Mary, and I'll lift him out."

This was done, and a little later Bert, in the arms of his father, was carried out of the cave, his mother following with the torch.

"Is he all right?" asked Mrs. Watson.

Bert, getting down out of his father's arms, answered for himself:

"Sure, I'm all right. What happened, anyhow?"

"You went into the cave, fell, and hit your head so hard that you fainted," his mother told him, while she parted his hair to look for a possible cut or gash.

"Oh, I remember now," Bert said, in a dazed sort of way, putting his hand to his head. "I felt myself falling and I yelled to Freddie so he wouldn't come in and get in the hole. Yes, I hit my head all right."

But it was nothing worse than this, and aside from a little cut on his scalp Bert suffered no injury. A drink of water and some more of the cool fluid on his head soon made him feel all right again.

"It isn't safe to go into a dark cave without a light, unless you know every step of the way," warned Mr. Bobbsey, as they went back to where Nan and Flossie had been left with the baby.

But before that was done Mr. Bobbsey explored the cave. He found that the recent rain had washed out a deep hole near the entrance, and it was this hole into which Bert had unsuspectingly stepped.

"Some one else may do the same thing," Mr. Bobbsey said. "I'll put some tree branches in front of the cave as a warning. Later we'll make a danger sign to fasten up over the entrance."

They found Nan and her sister anxiously waiting, and the two girls were relieved to find out that Bert wasn't hurt much.

Baby Jenny had awakened by this time, and as it was nearly noon Mrs. Bobbsey and Mrs. Watson decided to set out the picnic lunch, which was done on a flat stump within sight and sound of Buttermilk Falls.

"Don't eat too much, Bert," his mother warned him, as the good things from the basket were ready.

"Why not?" he asked.

"Because after a blow on the head you might be made ill if you ate too heartily."

"Oh, I'm all right," insisted the lad, with a brave little smile, though his head ached somewhat. "I didn't know what happened. I felt myself going down and I yelled and then I seemed to go to sleep."

The remainder of the day was passed

pleasantly in the woods. Later the other children were allowed to peer into the cave while their father held a torch that illuminated it.

"I wouldn't want to be a pirate and live there," said Nan with a shrug of her shoulders, as she turned away.

"Pirates don't mind the dark—they like it," said Freddie, as if he knew all about it.

The next day was a busy one, for many peaches had to be sorted to be taken to the auction market. The children rode to Hitchville again, for they liked the busy excitement of the place. It was well that Mr. Watson got a good quantity of his fruit over to Hitchville, for the following day it rained, when it would not have been wise to transport the peaches.

The rain storm was a hard one and, for midsummer, the day was raw and cold. As the Bobbsey twins could not go out, they managed to have fun in one of the barns. Sam Porter, who had gone fishing with Bert the day the bees swarmed, came over and taught the children some new games.

He and Bert decided to give a "circus act," as they called it. They made trapezes of bits of harness and some old broom handles and swung by their legs and arms.

"Watch me do the giant's turn!" cried Bert, as he took an especially long swing on the trapeze. But one of the straps broke, the end of the trapeze bar slipped down, and Bert had a fall.

"Oh!" cried the other children, as they saw the boy drop.

But Bert came to no harm, for the trapezes were over big, deep piles of hay, and he fell on one of these piles. Mr. Bobbsey, when he learned what sort of a game the boys were playing, had insisted that the hay be piled under the trapezes, for he was afraid lest they break.

"It's lucky that hay was there," Bert said. "I know now why they put nets under the high trapezes in the circus."

In the afternoon it had not cleared, and Nan, getting tired of playing in the barn, went back to the house. She heard Mrs. Watson saying to Mrs. Bobbsey:

"If I wasn't so busy I'd make some peach tarts. There are plenty of soft peaches that ought to be used."

"Oh, could I make the tarts?" begged

Nan. "I know how to make biscuits and I guess I could make tarts."

"I'll show you how," offered her mother, after Mrs. Watson had said Nan might use the kitchen.

"And I want to make some, too," put in Flossie.

"No, dear, you are too little," Nan replied. "But you can watch me, and, when you get a little older, you will know how."

"But I want to make some myself," insisted Flossie. However, they would not let her, so she had to be content to sit in a chair near the kitchen table and watch while Nan's mother showed her how to mix the dough and roll out the crust, cutting it into little circles which, when filled with cut-up peaches and baked, would be tarts.

But when Nan had a batch of the tarts ready to go into the oven, she left the kitchen a minute, and this was just the chance Flossie had been waiting for.

"I know how to make peach tarts," said the little girl to herself. "I'll show 'em I can make tarts just as good as Nan."

All the things Nan had used were on the table, flour, milk, mixing bowls, and the like. Flossie sifted some flour into a brown bowl, poured in some milk, added a little salt and lard, and then began to stir the mixture.

But she found that the table was too high for her to reach in comfort, even while standing on a chair.

"I'll set the bowl on the floor," decided Flossie. "Then I can stir my tarts and then I'll cut them out, like Nan did, and put in the peaches and bake 'em."

She lifted the bowl off the table and was climbing down out of the chair when suddenly she slipped. Just as Nan opened the door to come back and clean up, she saw Flossie fall to the floor with the bowl of dough.

Crash! What a sound it was!

"Oh!" cried Nan.

"Oh!" gasped Flossie.

And then you should have seen her!

CHAPTER XXII

HOME AGAIN

POOR Flossie Bobbsey seemed to be covered from head to foot with the dough she had mixed to make peach tarts as she had seen Nan doing. Of course there may have been a few spots on the little girl that were not covered with the mixture of flour and water, but there were not many. Flossie had made her dough "very sloppy," as Bert said, and it splattered all about. There was much on the floor, some on the chair, but most of it was on Flossie.

"Oh, you poor child! What in the world were you trying to do?" cried Nan, as she ran across the room to pick up her little sister.

"I was—now—I was makin' tarts!" sobbed Flossie. "Did I break Mrs. Watson's mixing bowl, Nan?" For her eyes were so filled with flour that she could not see out of them now.

"No, the bowl isn't broken," answered Nan kindly. "And I'll help you clean up, Flossie. Oh, but it is a terrible mess!" she sighed.

Mrs. Bobbsey and Mrs. Watson, hearing the crash of Flossie's fall, had run to the kitchen. They could tell at once what had happened, but Flossie thought it best to explain.

"I was making peach tarts," she said. "But I didn't finish."

"Never mind," soothed her mother, for Flossie had been punished enough, Mrs. Bobbsey thought. "You may have some of Nan's tarts."

And when Flossie had been washed and a clean dress put on her, she was given one of the first of the tarts from the oven. For Nan's baking turned out wonderfully well.

"You're getting to be quite a cook," complimented Mr. Watson at the table a little later, when Nan's tarts were served.

"You can put the story of Flossie and her tarts in your composition, Nan," suggested Bert.

"Yes, I guess I will," was his sister's answer. "I hope some more things happen around here before we go home," Nan went on. "The more things I have in my composition the better it will be, and maybe I can win the prize."

"I'd give some one a good prize if he or she could find my lost glasses," sighed Mrs. Martin. She was still without her spectacles, though she gave up a large part of each day to looking for them.

"I guess you'll have to wait until your doctor gets back, and then have him write you a prescription for a new pair," suggested Mr. Watson, as he got on the floor to "play horse" with Baby Jenny.

"I think some one must have taken them, either by mistake or on purpose," said the old lady. "I remember perfectly well that I had them the day the cattle ran away. Then I laid them down and some one must have come in and picked them up."

"Who would do such a thing as that?" asked Mrs. Bobbsey.

"Well, some of those cattle men might," Mrs. Martin answered. "Those were rough fellows, and they might take a notion to my glasses. The frames were of solid gold."

"But all the men who drove the cattle were

young fellows," said Mr. Watson. "None of them wore glasses."

"Well, I don't know," sighed Mrs. Watson's cousin. "I wish I had my glasses, that's all I can say."

The happy days at Cloverbank were drawing to a close. Mr. Bobbsey planned to take his family back home in about a week, so the children could resume their studies at school.

"But first I must get some more things to put in my composition," Nan said. "Are you going to work on yours, Bert?" she asked her brother, as she saw him wandering about the house as if searching for something. "Are you looking for a pencil and paper?"

"I'm looking for my pole," he said. "I'm going fishing with Sam. I have lots of time to write a composition after I get back to Lakeport."

"Oh, yes," agreed Nan. "I'm going to write my composition after I get home, but I want some things to happen here so I'll have plenty of incidents, as Miss Skell calls them."

In the days that followed the Bobbsey twins had much fun. They went on picnics to the woods and to Buttermilk Glen, but Bert kept away from the pirate's cave.

The children played in the barns, they helped feed the chickens and gathered the eggs. Old Speck came off her nest beneath the barn with a brood of ten little chickens and was put in a coop near the house. Flossie and Freddie devoted themselves to this little family, feeding them and giving them water every day.

When another crop of hay was gathered, the twins were allowed to ride on top of the loads as they were brought in from the field, though Nan did not again try to operate the trolley fork. Twice Bert and Sam went fishing, and once they took Freddie who, to his great delight, caught a good-sized chub. But it dropped off the hook when close to the bank and flapped its way back toward the creek.

"I'll get you! I'll get you!" shouted the little fellow, and he threw himself on the fish so vigorously that he slipped and went into the water himself. But Bert and Sam soon pulled him out.

The late crop of peaches was being picked when it was time for the Bobbsey family to return home. Mr. Bobbsey had gone to Lakeport to attend to some business, but was coming back to drive his family home in the automobile.

"Only one day more," sighed Nan, one afternoon, when word came in a letter that Mr. Bobbsey would arrive the following morning and that the twins must be ready to leave. "Oh, it's so wonderful here I could stay forever!"

"So could I," Bert said. "But at the same time I'll be glad to get back home and see the fellows. We're going to have a football eleven this season, and maybe I'll be captain."

"And I suppose I'll be glad to get home after I arrive," said Nan. "Anyhow, I want to see if I can win the composition prize. And that reminds me, I want to gather some yellow flowers I saw the other day and didn't know what they were. Miss Skell said we should put in something about the trees and the flowers we saw."

So Nan, taking Flossie and Freddie with her, went to gather the blossoms, so she could find out their name, while Bert went on a last fishing trip with Sam.

Bert came back from his trip with a fine string of fish which were cooked for the evening meal. Mr. Watson said he would miss this treat, as he was so busy he seldom had time to go to the creek with hook and line.

Early the next morning all was in readiness for the trip back to Lakeport. The Bobbsey twins, brown as berries from their life out of doors, once again put on their "good clothes," valises were packed, and the auto was brought to the door.

"Have you got room for these?" asked Mr. Watson, pointing to three baskets of choice peaches on the porch. "I sorted these out especially for you. They'll stand the journey, if you don't jounce them too much over the rough roads, and when you get them home, Nan, you can make some more tarts."

"Indeed we'll make room for the peaches!" said Mr. Bobbsey. "And very glad we are to have them"

"If we could take some bees home, we could have some honey, too," remarked Freddie.

They all laughed at this, and the farmer said:

"I'm afraid it would be dangerous to carry bees. But in the fall I'll send you some honey."

"Well, good-bye, folks!" called Zeek. "I've got to go back to the peach orchard. We're getting in the last load now and I don't want anything to happen to it."

The children and their parents said farewell to the kind hired man, and Mrs. Martin called after him:

"If you find my lost glasses anywhere, Zeek, bring them back with you."

"I will," he promised, though of course as she had lost them around the house, he would hardly find them in the orchard.

"Good-bye! Good-bye! Good-bye!" was called over and over again, Baby Jenny waving her little hand to the travelers. Then, with a jolly tooting of the auto horn, the Bobbseys began their homeward journey.

There was no delay and no such experiences as had befallen them on their trip to Cloverbank, although there was one detour that made, for a short time, a little rough going, and that evening they reached their home in Lakeport. Dinah and Sam were at the house, waiting to greet them.

"How's all mah honey lambs?" asked the fat cook, as she took some of the baggage Mrs. Bobbsey handed out.

"We're all well, thank you, Dinah," said Mr. Bobbsey. "Did you and Sam have a good vacation?"

"Jes' fine!" answered Sam.

"But Ah suah did miss de chilluns!" murmured Dinah. "Whut all am dis?" she asked as she saw the baskets in the car.

"Those are some peaches Mr. Watson gave us," said Mrs. Bobbsey.

"I'm going to make peach tarts," added Nan.

"I think those peaches had better be sorted," observed Mr. Bobbsey. "We went over a bit of rough road in making that detour, and some fruit may be bruised."

"That's right," agreed his wife. "And as Mr. Watson told us, a few bruised peaches in a basket may spoil the whole lot. We'll turn them out on the table and sort them." This work was begun as soon as the Bobbseys had rested a little while.

As the last peaches from one of the baskets rolled out on the table, Nan, looking in the bottom of the container, uttered a cry, darted out her hand, and said:

"Look! I've found Mrs. Martin's glasses!"

"Mrs. Martin's glasses!" exclaimed her mother. "Where were they?"

"In the bottom of that basket, covered with the peaches," said Nan. "Look!" She held out the spectacle case which, when it was opened, proved to contain the old lady's glasses, not in the least harmed.

"How did they get there?" asked Bert.

No one knew, of course, but it was thought that the empty peach basket must have been on the porch at the time of the cattle scare. Mrs. Martin must either have dropped or, in her excitement, have put the glasses in the basket. Later it was set out in the shed, no one looking to see if it contained anything. The glasses must have remained in the basket all the while, and even when the peaches were put in to be given to Mr. Bobbsey, no one saw the spectacle case. The case was about the color of the basket, and, of course, a spectacle case is not large.

"But here they are, safe, and how glad Mrs. Martin will be," said Mrs. Bobbsey. "I'll mail them right back to her."

This was done, and a grateful letter of thanks came in reply a few days later.

"Baby Jenny misses the children," Mrs. Watson had added in a postscript to her cousin's missive.

"And we miss her," said Nan. "But I've got something more to put in my composition —I'm going to write about the lost glasses and how they were found in the peaches."

School opened about a week later, and after the first few sessions Miss Skell brought up the subject of the vacation compositions. She gave the children three days in which to write and hand in their essays, and Nan worked hard. Bert also wrote one, but he spent so little time over it that his mother said he would not stand much chance of winning the prize.

At last the day came when the decision was to be made. There were some anxious hearts among the boys and girls in Miss Skell's class as the teacher faced them ready to tell who had won the prize.

"Most of you did very well," said their instructor. "Much better than I expected. There were some excellent compositions handed in—and some very poor and short ones." As she said this she seemed to look at Bert Bobbsey. "But the best of all was Nan Bobbsey's," went on Miss Skell. "So I award her the prize and I am going to ask her to come up here and read her composition to you. I think you will all enjoy it. The name of it is 'A Vacation in the Country.' Come, Nan."

Nan blushed, but, proud and happy, she read her story and the boys and girls all said it was most interesting. Nan told in an entertaining way about many of the incidents that had taken place at Cloverbank, and on the way there and back, just as they have been told to you here.

"Now what books do you want for a prize?" asked Miss Skell, when Nan had finished.

"A set of nice story books for girls, if you please," was the answer.

And that is what Nan received a little later. She still has those books, and thinks them the best in her little library.

"Well, we certainly had fun at Cloverbank," said Bert to his brother and sisters that afternoon on their way home from school, Nan hurrying to tell the good news about winning the prize.

"Lots of fun," she agreed.

"Wasn't it funny when Freddie and I saw the bear that turned into a calf?" laughed Flossie.

"And wasn't it fun that day when we played outdoors in the rain?" asked Freddie. "I wonder if we'll ever have fun like that again?"

Of course the children could not guess that they were to be very merry and laugh many times on their next vacation. It is told about in "The Bobbsey Twins at Cherry Corners."

"I'm going to play outdoors even when I'm big," said Flossie. "I just love it."

"When I grow up, I'm going to be a farmer," announced Freddie.

"Not a fireman?" Bert teased his brother.

"Well, maybe I can be a fireman in the wintertime," decided the little boy.

THE END